PETE & LILY

I can't take my eyes off Mom and Mr. Rosenblume. Yards ahead, they are jogging and talking and talking and jogging. Granted, she's a good enough runner, being a mother and all. This morning, though, her feet are flying out behind her! Also, she is laughing like crazy, and *I'd* like to know what's so darned funny.

"What's so funny?" Lily mutters, echoing my thoughts.

"I had no idea your father was such a comedian," I answer sarcastically.

"He's not," she says knowingly. "They're just giggling. I'll tell you one thing, though. There's *definitely* a touch of chemistry in the air."

"If your father's looking for chemistry, he better look somewhere else," I grump, tugging at loose red sweatpants. "My mom isn't available."

"And a new love affair for Henry is entirely out of the question."

Pete
and Lily

PETE & LILY

Amy Hest

A Beech Tree Paperback Book
New York

10 9 8 7 6 5 4 3 2 1

Library of Congress Cataloging-in-Publication Data

Hest, Amy.
    Pete and Lily/Amy Hest.
        p.   cm.
    Summary: When Pete's widowed mother starts dating Lily's divorced
father, the two girls decide they need to control the situation.
    ISBN 0-688-12490-9
    [1. Single-parent family—Fiction. 2. Apartment houses—Fiction.
3. Friendship—Fiction.]   I. Title.   II. Title: Pete & Lily.
[PZ7.H4375PE   1993]
[Fic]—dc20
                                                    92-42319
                                                        CIP
                                                         AC

For My Mom, With Love

CHAPTER

1

My name is Pete, but I'm not a boy. It's short for Patricia, although nobody calls me that. Well, hardly ever. Maybe in a couple of years, when I'm fourteen or fifteen and an official teenager, maybe then I will use Patricia all the time. But not yet.

Friday afternoon. Apartment 9B. I am fumbling for my keys as usual, digging into denim pockets, when the door swings open.

"Good news, Pete, Gram is coming!" My mother's tone is bright and those soft green eyes are nearly dancing.

I hang my nylon knapsack on the inside doorknob, then follow her through the beige-and-white living room and into the kitchen.

"She's flying in Sunday morning." Mom slides a long-edged knife off the magnetic wall rack. Like a short-order cook, she manipulates both hands to cut and balance, chopping an onion into fine little bits.

"Can we meet her at the airport?" I ask, ducking into the refrigerator.

"You bet."

I stand up straight and rub a McIntosh apple against the seat of my jeans. Biting into it with a squish, I start sculpting a narrow white ring around the middle. A visit from Gram! Now that's the nicest news I've heard in months. If there's one thing Mom and I could stand right now, it's a good dose of Gram's cheerful bossing.

"I'm cooking up her favorites," Mom says, *"ratatouille* and brisket." When she angles the chopping board, onion slivers by the hundred dive for the cast-iron pan heating on the stove.

"She better like deli sandwiches," I tease, "the *real* specialty of the house these days."

Mom turns from the stove. Holding her iced, un-spiked orange juice in one hand, she hoists herself onto the tall wood stool across from me. Manhattan kitchens are notoriously cramped, unless you happen to be rich. Which we aren't. So we do our eating at a rectangular butcher block attached to the wall with two brass hinges. Four matching bar stools slide underneath, to save space.

"I'm so glad she's coming." Mom smiles absently. "I suppose you're never too old to want some mothering."

As she plants her elbows on the table, that familiar glazed look sweeps across her face. She fidgets with the heavy collar of her turtleneck sweater, rolling it up, past the tip of her chin. Gold hoop earrings disappear into the navy blue wool. *You're so pale,* I would like to tell her.

2

May I suggest a little makeup? But I wouldn't suggest anything these days. She's not in the mood.

Besides, she looks okay even without makeup. Not that you're likely to mistake her for a movie star walking down Fifth Avenue. She has two best features—straight, sandy-colored hair and those gentle eyes that slant just a fraction. My father, who was slightly corny on the subject of my mom, used to boast that hers was a "classic face." And, he always took her picture.

"How long will Gram stay this time?"

"She didn't say." Mom's index finger is long and thin and just right for swirling ice cubes through her drink. They clink peacefully against the glass.

"Is this another business trip? Maybe she's coming to bawl out her stockbroker again!"

"Your grandmother wants to see that I meet a proper man," Mom reports without looking at me.

"A *what?*" I lean forward and search her eyes for a sign that she's kidding. "But you're not interested in meeting men!"

"Just try telling that to 'The Matchmaker of Park Avenue,'" Mom answers.

Matchmaker, my eye! I certainly will tell Gram, the minute she steps off that plane, my mother hasn't got the slightest snip of interest in going out with men. Impossible! After all, my father just died last January. Why she'd never even look at another man after loving him the way she did. And anyway, she wants to spend her free time with *me*.

"We'll remind Gram that matchmaking is hopeless in

a city like New York." I rotate the half-eaten apple in my hand.

Mom laughs. "We'll tell her to practice that particular skill of hers down in Miami."

Miami. I think about that chilly afternoon two winters ago when Gram told us she was moving to Florida. It must have been a Sunday, because we were watching some important football game when she stopped by. She arrived as she always did in the cold months, wrapped in her long raccoon coat and toting a box of raspberry-filled cookies from her fancy East Side bakery.

"I need a change," she announced smack in the middle of the fourth quarter. "So I've just sold the apartment, and I'm going south."

We switched off the game, but it was too late. Gram had really done it, sold her big Park Avenue apartment, the one my mom grew up in. And it seemed as if she was packed up and gone overnight.

Who could have guessed then how different our lives would be now? Who'd have guessed my father would have that heart attack and die on us?

As I pick away at the brownish apple core, three pits drop onto the table in front of me. I pinch together my thumb and third finger and each one flies straight across the kitchen . . . zing.

I stare at my favorite family snapshot, the Fire Island one propped against the electric coffeepot, and wonder for the hundredth time why we can't go back. Back to the nice times. When life was simple and Mom didn't rush off to an office every single day and my father was here, the way fathers ought to be, taking care of us. . . .

Suddenly I feel my lips slip into a tentative smile. Ninety-nine percent of the time I am just plain sad when I think about my father, because I miss him so much. But every once in a while, just as that unmistakable crummy feeling sinks toward my stomach, the funniest picture pops into my head. It's this image of him *chasing* people. Chasing them with that Swedish camera of his.

I can hear him now.

Very polite. "Would you mind, madam, if I took your boy's picture?" he would ask as he whipped my Frisbee halfway across The Sheep Meadow in Central Park. By the time I brought it back, he'd shot half a roll of film on some kid he didn't even know.

Or walking up Broadway in the middle of a downpour, he'd spin around and call out in that friendly low-pitched voice, "I'm with *City Magazine*! May I take your picture, sir, with the collie . . . ? Must be that red vinyl cape . . ."

Usually I tried to act as if he didn't belong to me, I was so embarrassed. Why couldn't he be like other fathers and mind his own business? Mom says he was a charmer though, and maybe he was, because time and again I watched total strangers blush and gush and fall all over themselves in order to please "the famous photographer."

Not me, though..

"Pete! You *exasperate* me!" he would say, shaking his

head from side to side. "I spend half my life taking pictures of people whose names I don't know, and my own daughter won't sit still for a minute. . . ."

But some things you just can't help. Whenever that classy camera was focused on me, I felt so silly and inadequate. And plain. Something inside would make me turn away, screw up my nose, squirm like a two-year-old, or simply take off. If only he'd come back, I would let him take my picture any time he wanted. I would sit still for hours at a clip. If only he'd come back.

"Wake up, Pete!" Mom's hand is waving in front of my eyes. "You're a million miles away," she adds, looking worried.

"I'll make up the bed for Gram." I pat her hand, then unwrap my legs from the skinny ones of the bar stool.

My room faces Central Park, a stroke of extraordinary good luck. To live in this city and not have your bedroom flush up against a brick wall is the height of luxury. New Yorkers go crazy for views, and especially the one from my window, for Central Park—no matter what people say about the muggers and creeps who hang out there—is a splendid sight.

I stand at the window, pushing my nose flat against the cold pane. November already. Overnight, it seems, the leaves have turned their pretty orange and yellow, their purples and shades of red. The sky is more dark than light and a blustery wind makes the clouds glide quickly overhead.

"You can't make a bed without these." Mom's voice makes me jump. She is half-hidden behind a pile of

6

sheets, the new ones with stripes, and the soft white blanket Gram loves.

I smile and take them from her. "Good teamwork, Mom."

"I don't know what I'd do without you." She sighs softly and pulls me close. "It's been some rough year, hasn't it, Pete?"

"But we're okay now." I say it with my strong voice, but it's a fake. *I want my father! It's no fair!* And I cling to her, swallowing at my tears and wanting her all to myself, always.

What was it Gram said last time she was here, in August for my birthday? The voice on the other side of Mom's bedroom door was hushed but firm.

"It's time to start picking up the pieces, Ellen. For your sake and Pete's, you need to pull yourself together and get on with your life."

As I watch her now, those mellow eyes looking past me to the treetops out my window and beyond, I wonder how long it takes a person to pick up the pieces, how long it takes to get on with your life.

Some people, I suppose, are better at it than others.

CHAPTER

2

Lily Rosenblume is my best friend. She lives right downstairs in 2E with her father and her brother Jake, who is four and adorable. Her parents are divorced, although this one is a little unusual because the kids live with Mr. Rosenblume and it's their mother who gets the visiting rights with a schedule.

Lily and Jake spend most vacations on a ranch in Wyoming. Near Cheyenne. That's where Mrs. Rosenblume, who is now called Mrs. Carey-Jones, is living these days. Lily calls her mom's new husband The Cowboy, but I've seen his picture and he doesn't really look like one.

Mom and I have just polished off a couple of salami sandwiches when Lily raps on the kitchen door.

"Hi guys." She slinks into the room.

Mom slides off the kitchen stool and walks around her slowly, once, twice, squinting finally as she holds Lily's fine pointed chin in her hand. "Mascara?"

Lily smiles. "Do you like it, Mrs. Jaffe?"

Mom wraps her arm around Lily's narrow waist, a gesture at once maternal and chummy. "Pretty glamorous," she admits, "although I think your lashes are plenty long without it."

"Woolworth's had a special," Lily explains. What she doesn't explain is that *I* loaned her the dollar fifty. As usual. With the promise that I could use it anytime I want.

As if my mother would let me! Growing up. The whole subject, from mascara to boys, makes her kind of jumpy lately. Probably she's beginning to realize I'm on the verge of doing it. Not that I'm in any great hurry. And especially where boys are concerned.

Lily's another story, though. Take last Sunday. She walked over to the Metropolitan Museum of Art with Mom and me. Mom looked at the paintings. Lily looked at the boys. And I looked at Lily, just to see how she gets boys to flirt with her. In a thousand years I couldn't do what she does!

She stood beside an older boy with a backpack on his shoulder and a sketch pad in his hand, watching the painting he was watching on the white wall in front of them.

"Interesting blend of color," I heard her whisper, right into his ear.

The backpack boy turned and leaned toward her. "Are you from Paris?" he asked. "You look French or something."

When we got home, Mom let me know what was on

9

her mind. "Lily is getting too wise for her years," she said.

"How? What do you mean?"

So she tried to put some complicated theory (probably something she read in one of those fat psychology books on the shelf above her bed) into mothery words.

"Lily is racing ahead," she began cautiously. "I sometimes think she's forgotten how to be a little girl."

"We've been little girls long enough," I said. "Twelve years is plenty."

In secret though, I *am* worried that Lily *is* racing ahead, socially I mean. She reads *New York Magazine* and *Seventeen*. Her father takes her to the ballet twice a year and to elegant city restaurants one night a month. Lily can whip off the subtleties of *suprême de volaille à blanc* and *suprême de volaille à brun* about as easily as I can describe the difference between chocolate and chocolate-chip ice cream.

"Believe me, I'd rather stuff myself at the Spaghetti Factory," she insists, "or McDonald's."

"Then how about trading places?" I suggest. "You stay home for scrumptious deli sandwiches and your father can drag me, kicking and screaming, to *Le Bœuf*."

Mom hands Lily a glass of milk. "What's new?" she asks.

"Well, Henry's got a new *friend*," Lily says in that smirky-sarcastic tone of voice that means her father's *friend* is a girl friend.

"What is this one's name?" I ask.

"Nina something-or-other." Lily makes a face.

10

"If you ask me, your father has too many girl friends," I comment, licking mustard off the side of my finger.

"Would you believe she's called looking for him three times in the last two hours!" Lily closes her eyes to show her displeasure.

"I would believe it, " I say.

"Well, Nina better learn there are some ground rules when it comes to dating Henry Rosenblume," Lily warns.

"And what are those?" Mom wants to know.

"First of all, he's got two kids to take care of. Second, he's overworked at his job . . ." Lily sighs. "I don't know why they run after him. All he worries about is his beautiful body. Like he'd die of flabby wrists or something if he forgot to work out two days in a row."

Mom laughs. "You mustn't be surprised, Lily, that women chase after your father."

"Why?"

"He's not only available, but very handsome. As a matter of fact," she jokes, "I wouldn't mind dating him myself."

"Mother!" I groan. "That isn't funny." I turn to Lily. "Now, what about the third thing?" I ask, chipping away at the words.

Lily looks directly at my mother a moment before she speaks. "Ground rule number three," she says slowly, "is when it comes to dating Henry, all those women better understand, right from the start, the relationship hasn't got a prayer."

"Why not?"

"Because I think my parents are getting back together again."

"Together?" Mom scrunches up her eyebrows.

"Your mother is remarried, Lily, to The Cowboy!" I exclaim.

"My mother," she responds calmly, "is still married to my father. In her heart, I mean."

Now the way I look at things, you're either married or you're not married. Lily's parents definitely are not. Nor have they been for two years. Two years ago is when her mother decided she loved Carl Carey-Jones more than she loved Henry Rosenblume.

"That's crazy!" Mom is saying.

"There are statistics, Mrs. Jaffe. Divorced couples have been known to get back together."

"They have?" I say.

"Just listen to this letter from my mother." Lily pulls two sheets of lavender paper from her patch pocket. She runs her finger down the second page and starts reading out loud.

Darling Lily,

I bet you were a great wicked witch in the school play, although I think you're far too pretty for that role! And thanks, honey, for taking Jake trick-or-treating. I feel so bad that I'm not sharing these special moments with you.

12

Lily looks up. "What do you think, Mrs. Jaffe?"

"I think she misses you."

"I think she feels guilty," I say. "All the divorced parents I know live right across town from each other, not a million miles away in Wyoming."

"Pete!" Mom reprimands.

"That's all right, Mrs. Jaffe." Lily shrugs. "Pete knows, my mom belongs here. But I think it's *guilt* that will bring her back home again."

Mom frowns. "Your mother and Henry have chosen different roads, Lily. . . ."

"Can we talk about this some other time?" I cut in, suddenly impatient. "We need to start those English compositions, Lily."

"First the dishes. Would you mind, girls?" Mom fills the sink with hot water, then squirts green detergent. She looks upset. "I'm going out for a walk," she says, quickly leaving the room.

Lily's eyes and mine lock for a second, but we don't say a word. My mother's night walks have been known to go on for hours. She calls it her thinking time, but from the swollen nose and red eyes, it is pretty obvious that it's also her crying time. The worst part is not knowing if she'll come back in ten minutes or two hours. And I'll never forget that night last May, the night I found myself—exhausted from the waiting—banging pathetically on the Rosenblumes' door.

"She's gone!" I wailed into Mr. Rosenblume's thick chest.

"Your mother is walking," he murmured, his voice smooth as velvet, "just walking."

"Shouldn't we call the police," I shuddered miserably, "Missing Persons or something?"

And then we laughed, for Mr. Rosenblume *is* the police. He's a detective, pretty high and mighty too, with the New York City Police Department.

"Your mom needs this time." He stroked my head. "It isn't easy for her."

"She misses my father so much."

"Of course."

Across the room, Lily pokes around the freezer. "What's to eat?" she asks, absently twisting her long ponytail around a forefinger. Deepest black and stick straight, hers is the kind of hair movie stars ought to have, not regular kids.

Lucky Lily. She's beautiful. Until recently I never gave it a second thought. She was always the pretty one and I wasn't, and that was that. But now as I watch her, it strikes me again that it's only a matter of time before boys start calling her for dates. Real dates.

As a matter of fact, there is already a boy in her life. I wouldn't call him a boyfriend in the conventional sense, but he does go out of his way at least once a day to talk to her. And he's not just any boy either. Roger Starr is the cutest eighth grader at P.S. 7. Everybody knows it too! There isn't a girl in school who doesn't swoon when he walks by.

Of course Lily, being Lily, says she doesn't give a hang about *cute*. She says a person's character is what counts.

Me? I'll take cute. Except not yet.

I stack the last dishes on the drain board near the sink. Lily decides finally on a small rectangular chocolate cake and places it on the edge of the table. She unseals the red cardboard lid, smacking her lips in anticipation.

"Save me half of that icing," I warn, pulling myself onto the stool next to her and checking out her new skirt.

While most kids our age dress pretty much the same, in jeans of varying states of fade, Lily has an unusual flair for style. She prowls the secondhand shops along Columbus Avenue like some sleuth, occasionally raising enough cash to buy an "antique" dress or blouse. Last year I nearly died when she presented me with an ancient brocade change purse for my birthday.

"It's genuine!" Her eyes were bright with pride. "A turn-of-the-century, one-of-a-kind piece."

"I love it," I lied, turning it over and over in my hands, wondering why she couldn't give me a normal present.

Now if *I* ever showed up at P.S. 7 in a long silky dress that buttoned down the back, I'd be laughed out the front door. But nobody laughs at Lily. Instead, girls crowd around to touch and admire the lacy collar and drippy fabric of her latest find.

Mom says Lily has a need to call attention to herself. Maybe she's right. Like tonight. Just to come up here, she is decked out in a colorful patchwork skirt that hangs around her ankles, and a nubby red turtleneck that must be her father's. She looks sixteen—especially with mascara.

Not me. I look twelve. Not twelve and a half or even twelve and a quarter. Just twelve. My hair isn't glamour-girl black, rather plain dark auburn, hanging in waves to my shoulders. I am not fashionably tall or exceptionally skinny. And those freckles that may have been cute when I was three are still splattered across the most babyish turned-up nose.

Lily dips a butter knife into the thick fudgy topping. She scrapes around all four sides until a gob of chocolate hangs on the edge of the blade. Aiming for her mouth, she clamps her lips around the fudge-coated knife, then slides it out again. My sophisticated Lily.

"Pete, who do you think is the cutest boy in school?"

"Everybody *knows* it's Roger Starr," I say.

Lily grins. Carving out a small chocolate cylinder from the middle of the cake, she hands it to me. "And who's second cutest?"

I shrug.

"Think, Pete. Who's second cutest?"

I think but no one comes to mind. "Who?"

"Jon Hill."

"Hm." I nod. "Doesn't he hang out with Roger?"

"He happens to be Roger's best friend." Lily says, twirling her ponytail around her finger. "Wouldn't it be great," she goes on dreamily, "if Jon liked you?"

"Me?"

"Well, what if Roger Starr was my boyfriend. Imagine how much fun it would be for his best friend to be *your* boyfriend!"

16

"You know I'm not interested in boys," I say, my throat suddenly dry.

"You're practically a teenager, Pete. It's time you got interested."

"Forget it." I laugh nervously, then push two notebooks across the table. "Let's get going. I'll write you a great lead sentence, Lily, if only you'll put that cake away."

She dips her finger one last time. "I wouldn't be surprised," she says with a slow smile, "if Jon Hill likes chocolate as much as you do."

Hunched over my paper, I write my name in script, then the date. "Very funny," I mutter without looking up.

But even as I say the words, I can't help wondering how it would feel if the second cutest boy in school happened to be your boyfriend.

CHAPTER

3

"Wake up, Mom."

No response.

"Time to get up!" I sing, tying a double knot on the drawstring designed to hold up baggy sweatpants. "You promised you'd come for a jog with me." I bend toward the squished pillow she's pulled over her head and whisper, "The exercise will be good for you, Princess."

"No fair," she grunts in her hoarse wake-up voice. "Even a princess needs her beauty sleep on Sunday morning."

"There's no time for that today. Gram's plane lands at ten." I sit on the big bed and pass her a steamy cup of black coffee, fresh-brewed in our old electric pot. "This will get you going."

"Mmmm, good coffee." She leans on an elbow, watching me and sipping quietly. "Like Daddy's."

That's because he taught me how to make it. I stand abruptly and smooth green leg warmers over my thighs.

"Cold weather is no excuse for falling apart," I say as she kicks at the blanket and swings her feet to the floor. "We need to keep in shape, Mom."

"What's this *we* business?" she answers. "I've been jogging three mornings a week for years and I happen to think I'm in very good shape!" She leans forward to examine her face in the little round mirror on her dresser. "No serious wrinkles this morning," she reports, "and with a little effort, I can still touch my toes. See!" She flops over at the waist.

Mom is right. She is in pretty good shape for someone who's pushing forty. Thin, but not skinny, she's a far cry from those fancy women who spend half their lives at the spa. Besides, she loves ice cream and gooey cakes as much as I do. She eats it openly too, and without guilt. Spa ladies eat all that stuff anyway, but they do it on the sly, then whine to each other about their cellulite. My mother doesn't even know what cellulite is.

Anyway, the fanciest thing about her is the pair of red-framed glasses I helped talk her into buying a couple of months ago. "A little pizzazz," the toothy salesman at Eyes Are You had coaxed. "You could stand just a touch of pizzazz."

For some reason grown-ups like to say I'm the spitting image of my mother. They're wrong. I look just like my father. The little boy's picture in a silver frame beside Mom's side of the bed proves it too. I don't wear glasses but if I did they would be wiry (like his) and California trendy. My hair is more red (like his) than blond and my complexion, all freckled up the way it is, doesn't begin to resemble Mom's, which is powdery pale. The one thing we do have in common, though, is eyes—so exactly the same shade of green my father used to say the color was blended in a single pot of paint.

"Where does this burst of energy come from, Pete?" Mom punches both arms through the sleeves of her hooded sweatshirt.

"Mr. Rosenblume's been making a bigger than usual fuss about keeping fit," I explain. "He says Lily and I are lazy, that we ought to be jogging three or four times a week."

"Then why isn't *Lily* running this morning?" she asks cheerfully.

"Lily's motto of the month happens to be 'Thou shalt not jog on Sunday.'"

Mom laughs. "What a character!"

Lily is a character. Everyone knows that. What she isn't is an athletic person. Once in a while I manage to talk her into jogging around with me, just for kicks. But it sure isn't the biggest issue in our lives. If we happen to be in the mood, we go, and if we don't happen to be in the mood, then there's always tomorrow.

On the other hand, Lily's father is downright compulsive about his exercise. He runs every single morning, including Sunday, in every kind of weather, including blizzards. He goes to the YMCA on Sixty-third Street to work out and swim laps. He even rides a bike to his precinct across town.

"I'm ready." Mom steps out of the bathroom. A bright

red bandanna is tied around her head to keep loose strands of hair from flopping in her face.

"It's about time!" I tease, ushering her toward the elevator. "By the way, thanks for the loan." I pat the pale pink ski vest she lets me wear from time to time. It looks especially good with washed-gray sweats.

Mom pulls the zipper up to my chin, then kisses the tip of my nose. "This one's my favorite too," she says with a sigh. "Perfect for weekends in Vermont."

She's talking about the old days, when she and my father would drive to some mysterious country inn for ski weekends all through the winter months. I never went along. They said it was their special time together. I wasn't crazy about being left behind, but the good part was I usually got to go to Gram's for a double overnight. What fun we had, and the delicious secrets we kept from my parents! One time she even took me to a disco in Soho.

Just as we are stepping out of our doorway, a kid swerves his bike in front of us, somehow hooking a handlebar onto Mom's sweatshirt.

"Hold it!" she shouts. "We're caught!"

He stops short and springs off the bike. Wouldn't you know, it's Jon Hill, the second cutest boy in P.S. 7—and my mother's yelling at him!

Jon notices me and looks petrified. Mom's sweatshirt has a raggedy zigzag sort of tear on the sleeve. I turn away. Maybe he'll forget I'm here. I cross my fingers, all of them, hoping against hope she won't start yelling again.

21

"There." She is untangled. "Next time be more careful."

He mumbles something into his chest, then pedals off. Fast.

"*That* was Jon Hill."

"And *who* is Jon Hill?" she asks, inspecting her sleeve.

So I tell her, shaking my head, wondering if the day will ever come when I can look a boy in the eye.

"First or second cutest," Mom says, "he should watch where he's going."

'Did you have to yell at him, Mom?"

"I didn't yell at him and if I did, he deserved it." Mom runs in place as we wait for the light to change at Seventy-second Street. "I'm freezing, Pete!"

"Then let's go in *there*," I point to the hundred-year-old Dakota apartments behind us. "I bet there's a fireplace in every room, and lavish Oriental carpets—"

"Daddy's favorite building," she interrupts. "He always said he'd like to spend his first million on an apartment there."

"And he took about a hundred pictures of it," I remind her. "Plenty of famous people live there, don't they?"

She nods absently.

Ours is a newer and less elegant building a couple of blocks south of The Dakota. There's nobody famous there, except you might say Mom was once kind of a celebrity. That's because way back when she was in college, she wrote a book that was on the best-seller list two weeks in a row.

"Will you ever write another best-seller?" I sometimes ask.

"First we pay the rent. Then we can talk best-sellers."

To pay the rent, she works at *Woman's World Magazine*. Before my father died, she was part-time fashion editor. Once in a while, in those days, I caught her unlocking the cabinet beside her bed to pull out manuscript pages from a book she must have been working on. But I guess it never did get written. And now her job is full-time, or full-time plus. Between the tons of paper she lugs home from her office every night, and the hysterical-sounding phone calls that follow, there isn't much time left over for writing books or anything else. Including me.

Leaving the city behind, we head down a curving ramp to the mainstream of the park. The quiet is sudden and imposing. I rub an icy nose with the palm of my hand and wriggle toes, already numbing, inside thick-soled running shoes.

Central Park joggers have several popular paths to choose from. Probably the prettiest run of all is around the Reservoir, with its early-morning city vistas in shades of pink and yellow. Since we live farther downtown, Mom and I usually stick to the so-called lower loop. Into the park at Seventy-second Street . . . down to Fifty-ninth . . . heading gradually toward the East Side, past the Carousel and sailboat lake, Bethesda Fountain and the rowboat lake . . . and up to West Seventy-second. Once around is nearly two miles. Nothing to sneeze at.

I pull up my elbows and start to run.

"Hey you!" Mom calls out before I've gone five yards. "How about a couple of stretches?"

"I hate warming up."

"Tough. If you want to be a runner, you do it right." She is fixed beside a tall golden tree. Leaning toward it until her outstretched hands touch the trunk, she bends one leg . . . slowly . . . then the other . . . ball, toes, heel, ball, toes, heel. . . .

Around the other side of the fat trunk, I mimic her. Loud sighs. "How am I doing, Mom?"

"Quit horsing around." She is folded over at the waist, legs apart, swinging arms and torso until the left palm brushes her right foot, right palm brushes left foot. Again and again.

Finally we run. Slowly at first. As we pick up speed, a natural kind of rhythmic breathing takes over. The books say you ought to be able to chat with your partner while you jog, but keeping up with my mother is next to impossible.

For all her complaints about getting out of bed, she breezes along as if she hasn't got a care in the world. She grins and waves to a couple of lovey-dovey tourists in a horse-drawn carriage. She turns little circles, her eyes fixed not on the pavement as mine are, but on the high handsome buildings that fringe the park. She breathes effortlessly and if I lag, which I do a lot, she swings around playfully, running backwards until I catch up.

"You're doing fine," she coos in that encouraging mother voice as I struggle past the Sixty-seventh Street

24

playground. I try to ignore the scrawny gray squirrel sunbathing on the kiddy slide.

As runners whip by, I try to figure out where they get their stamina. These are not exactly Olympic stars we're talking about either. Just everyday, run-of-the-mill New Yorkers. Most of them are twice my age and plenty are even older than my mother! Yet they move along with an ease and skill that make me feel like a first-class clodhopper. Me, with the cramp in my stomach that won't go away.

"Good morning!" Henry Rosenblume, in shapeless blue running pants and a bright orange sweatshirt labeled COP ON THE RUN, falls into step beside us. His black hair is beginning to go gray at the temples, I notice, and the skinniest line of sweat keeps dripping, then disappearing, into the stubby beard he's recently started to grow. The beard was Lily's idea. She's convinced it will make him look more dignified.

"Hello, Henry." Mom smiles. "You know, it's *your* fault I'm out here at seven on a Sunday morning," she tells him in the friendliest kind of voice.

"It is?"

"Your physical fitness mania is rubbing off," she says, "or at least *somebody* has been making sermons to Pete that go like this: 'Cold weather is no excuse for falling apart.'"

"Did I say that?" Mr. Rosenblume looks at me and winks. "Notice the effect my sermons have on Lily. She's asleep!"

"Sunday is Lily's day of rest," I explain with a straight face.

Mr. Rosenblume frowns.

"How many miles are you running these days?" Mom asks him.

"Six."

"Six!" She whistles. "I'm pretty impressed."

"Don't be." He runs alongside her. I wonder if he knows he practically stepped on my foot just now. "If I were playing shortstop for the Yankees," he jokes, "well, then you'd have good reason to be impressed."

"No need to be modest," Mom kids right back. "Not with me, Henry."

While these two are enjoying their cutesy little conversation, I am trying like crazy to keep up. But the more they chat, the faster they go. And the faster they go, the more annoyed I get. For a moment I picture myself whizzing past them on a skinny ten-speed bike, like Jon Hill's. . . . We swing around the sailboat lake, near Fifth Avenue. No boats this morning, still too early, but a big curly pooch is splashing on the top step. I call out to Mom to tell her, since *she's* the dog lover in the family, but she's yards ahead and can't hear me. *"This happens to be my time with my mother!"* I say it under my breath, but maybe Mr. Rosenblume will get the message if I concentrate hard enough.

A few minutes later Mom and I are trudging up the hill to Seventy-second Street. Mr. Rosenblume waves before he charges uptown to run a couple of laps around the Reservoir. It's about time he leaves us alone.

"Nice guy," Mom says in a soft swoon-voice.

"What's news about that?" I demand. "You've known Henry Rosenblume since Lily and I were little kids, and he's always been a nice guy. Big deal!"

"Don't pout, Pete. It's very unbecoming."

I don't answer because of course it's unbecoming to pout. I know that. Sometimes, though, a person just can't help herself.

CHAPTER

4

Flight Number Seven, nonstop Miami to New York, delayed one hour. To pass the time we've been dawdling over trinkets in the expensive little airport shops that sell everything from chewing gum to designer wallets. Mom is in a great mood. She even lets me buy some wild socks in purple silk for Lily and red ones for myself.

Gram arrives at last and I can't stop hugging her. After the usual ooohs and aaahs on the subject of my growing up, she gently disentangles herself and reaches for my mother.

"Ellen," she says, the slightest catch in a voice that is always so matter-of-fact.

"I'm so glad you're here," Mom practically whispers.

We link arms and glide through the maze of travelers and greeters in the overheated airport corridor.

"I suspect you will grow into those feet," Gram teases, pointing to my running shoes. "Well, at least you won't be short like me."

"I wish I could be pretty like you, Gram."

"Nonsense! You are plenty pretty."

When it comes to looking good though, Lee Remsen really takes the cake. Everyone says so, not just me. Her charcoal-gray hair, cut short and set each night in funny plastic rollers, is striking against the same pale, wrinkle-free skin Mom has. She isn't pudgy like most grandmothers either, but is thin and erect and you'd never guess she's already in her sixties. Also, she wears very expensive clothes that mostly come in lavender boxes from Bergdorf Goodman.

Mom says Gram has had a distinguished male following over the years. In other words, plenty of boyfriends. But even though my grandfather died long before I was born, she never remarried. "I need to come and go as I please," she reminds us often enough.

We climb into the backseat of a cab. As it bumps and jerks us onto the Grand Central Parkway, Gram turns to Mom. "You look awful," she says. "Are you getting any sleep at all?"

Now there's my grandmother for you. Instead of saying something touching and mothery like, "Poor Ellen! It's so very hard to be alone, without the husband you love," she twists everything around, as if my mother's happiness hinged on a good night's sleep.

Mom falls right into the trap, too. As if talking about her sadness would be a sign of weakness. "If I look exhausted, then here's the culprit," she says with a smile. "Pete's latest campaign is to drag me out of bed on *Sunday* for a predawn jog!"

"Running is bad for your knees," Gram warns. "I've been telling you that for years."

"But it's good for every other part of you," Mom protests, winking at me. "I've been telling *you* that for years!"

"On the other hand," Gram continues thoughtfully, "I've heard jogging is a chic new way for single people to meet. Have you met anyone, Ellen?"

"You mean *male* people?" Mom is trying not to smile.

"Of course, I mean male people!" Gram sighs. "Oh well, I suppose it's just another fad."

I shake my head. "Jogging is here for keeps."

"Maybe we'll even get *you* out there," Mom threatens.

"I plead senior citizen!"

"But there are plenty of seniors in the park, Gram." I can't keep from giggling. The thought of my grandmother in sweatpants. . . .

A couple of minutes later, we are skimming across the Triborough Bridge. The jagged skyline is bold and beautiful, and the city that stretches before us sparkles in the morning light.

"I miss you, New York," Gram murmurs.

"New York misses you, too." Mom hugs her for the tenth time.

After lunch I pile dishes in the sink and head for Lily's. Gram and Mom need their time together, and frankly, my ears are tired from all the chatter. We've been home since eleven-thirty, and they haven't stopped talking for a single minute. It seems to me those two can skip parts of sentences and understand each other anyway.

I run down the back stairs two at a time. The Rosenblumes' door is still decorated with the paper pumpkin Jake's nursery-school teacher dropped off on Halloween. She had the most pathetic crush on Mr. Rosenblume. But of course he was all tied up with Polly Struthers in October . . . or was it Molly what's-her-name?

Jake pulls open the door. "Lily went out for the newspaper," he announces, then swings around to call out, "Pete's here!" Straight brown hair flops around his ears and halfway over his dark round eyes.

"You need a haircut, Jake."

Mr. Rosenblume steps into the wide foyer. "I'll give him one tonight," he promises.

For a minute I consider telling him how he managed to ruin *my* run with *my* mother this morning. I don't have the guts though, and follow him instead, toward the back end of the apartment. He is wearing a navy T-shirt labeled COP IN THE KITCHEN. Very appropriate, since the Rosenblumes practically live in theirs, which is bigger and sunnier than ours. And there's enough gourmet equipment in here to please Manhattan's fanciest chefs. Lily says her dad keeps the stuff around to impress his girl friends.

"Would you mind giving me a hand with these dishes?" he asks, knowing very well I wouldn't dare mind. "I'm on my way to the office for a couple of hours. One more emergency in the Big Apple," he adds.

31

"I'm going with you!" cries Jake.

Mr. Rosenblume crouches down until he is eye level with his son. "Not today, honey."

"Oh yes." The tone is four-year-old stubborn as he crisscrosses his arms over that narrow chest. "I am too going."

"I'll baby-sit," I volunteer cheerfully. "We'll have a good time, Jake, like we always do."

Mr. Rosenblume gives Jake a quick hug, lifting him off the ground and thanking me with his eyes. "Now don't break your neck in here," he warns, tossing me the dishtowel.

I laugh knowingly. Jake collects miniature cars and trucks, and I mean dozens. They are everywhere. Underfoot for sure, they also stretch in zigzag rows across chairs; they dangle from white Formica counters and stick halfway out from the bottom of the refrigerator. Using colorful blocks and anything else from cookie sheets to vacuum-cleaner bags, Jake builds elaborate highways and tunnels, bridges and mountain passes, from here to his bedroom.

"Have a cookie, they're homemade," Mr. Rosenblume says, rushing from the room.

I take one from the flat red tin. And another. "Your sister sure turns out a decent chocolate-chip cookie," I tell Jake as he settles into my lap.

"She learned everything from her mother." Mr. Rosenblume is back in a tweed business jacket. "Those two used to spend hours at their baking—mostly chattering away, I think. . . . Lily misses that. . . ."

"I know she does." I sigh.

He pauses in the middle of knotting his tie, and a queer sad look sweeps across his face. But then it's gone, covered over by one of those phony adult smiles that means it's time to change the subject.

"My grandmother's here," I say, flashing him a pretty phony smile of my own and wondering if maybe Mr. Rosenblume still misses his wife in spite of all those girl friends. "But Mom says Gram came with a mission."

"What's that?"

"I think she wants to make my mother start going out. With men, I mean."

Mr Rosenblume laughs. "Mothers! They're all the same."

Jake and I walk him to the front door. I hold it open with the side of my foot. In the public hallway outside the apartment, he pokes impatiently at the elevator button.

"Remind Lily I'll be home by four, would you, Pete?"

"Right."

"By the way, how's your mother?"

What a dumb question! *You know very well how my mother is,* I want to tell him, since you decided to tag along with us just this morning. And besides, you must run into her fifty times a week—in the elevator, at the corner deli, down in the basement laundry room. . . . "She's fine," I mumble. Then I shut the door and hurry down the hall to Jake's cubicle of a room.

We are putting the finishing touches on a tall block castle when Lily barges in. Balancing the fat Sunday papers in the crook of her arm, she stops short in the doorway.

"We have to talk, Pete. *Alone.* I have two important things to tell you."

Jake bolts for the door yelling, "She's playing with me, Lily!"

"Don't be dumb. Pete does not come down here to play with a baby."

"I'm not a baby!"

Poor Jake. Poor me! Lily does an about-face and stomps out of the room. I know she expects me to follow. That's when Jake decides to collapse across my outstretched legs. "You're staying with me, right, Pete?" he pleads.

Lily reappears in the doorway to tell me the first important thing. "Roger Starr called."

"On the *phone?*" My voice is a squeak.

"He's coming over this afternoon."

I stare at Lily. "Why?"

"Why?" she repeats gaily. "Because he likes me!"

I try to smile and be gracious, really I do. But deep inside I'm already stuck with this other feeling, a nasty mean one called jealous. Roger Starr called Lily, and nobody called me. Roger Starr likes Lily, and nobody likes me. This is the beginning of the end of a beautiful friendship; I know it. Lily will *never* have time for boys *and* a best friend like me.

"Is Roger Starr big or little?" Jake is saying. "Will he play with me?"

"Sure," Lily answers absently. Then she takes a step

34

toward me and touches my shoulder. "Now I am going to tell you the second important thing. It's about my father."

"Your father?"

Lily nods. "He's been asking questions about your mother, Pete, all day long!"

"So what," I say, brooding still about Roger.

"Oh, he was cool enough," Lily goes on, "but I know Henry better than anyone, and I'm telling you . . . he is *smitten*. With a capital *S*."

"Smitten!" I repeat with a nervous laugh. "Your father . . . my mother . . . impossible!" Hard as I try to dismiss Lily's latest craziness, a tiny twinge of doubt settles in my stomach. I look her directly in the eye though, and tell her in my strong voice, "*You* are hallucinating, pal. With a capital *H*."

CHAPTER
5

This is it. No more stalling around. Tonight I'm going to have my talk with Gram. I've been putting it off all week. *Gram, you've got to help me,* I will tell her. *My mother isn't ready to meet men. She hasn't gotten over my father yet and neither have I.*

"Comfortable, Gram?" I begin.

"Very cozy." She smiles from her bed across the room.

"It's your favorite winter blanket," I remind her.

"Warm as toast."

I reach across the night table, behind the twisted pile of paperback books and fashion magazines, to switch off the lamp. Flowery sheets are supposed to make me think of spring, but tonight they are freezing cold and I kick at them in search of a warm spot.

I clear my throat. "Good night!"

"Sweet dreams, Pete." Her newspaper makes a muffled crinkly sound when she folds it over to zero in on an article. "Does the light bother you?"

I shake my head. "I like it. I like having you here," I add pleasantly, "watching me sleep."

"And I like being here."

"Talk about sleep, Gram, how do you get any with those things jabbing at your head? Don't they have hair-blowers down in Florida?" I tease.

She laughs absently, tapping the tips of her fingers across the pink forest of plastic rollers. "I'm trying to read," she scolds cheerfully. "Go to sleep!"

"Gram?"

"Yes?"

"I need to talk to you. It's about my mother."

"Well?"

It's just that—"

"Yes, Pete. Go ahead!"

So I blurt it out, without taking a breath once. "Mom does not want to meet men. She has her job to keep her busy, and she's got me for company. That's plenty."

Gram takes a breath. Then she says, "Your mother is young and vivacious. She's loving and she's bright. And, she's my daughter, Pete. I worry about her now the same as when she was your age."

"But she's a grown-up!"

"Doesn't matter," Gram insists.

"You know," I say quietly, "she still cries about Daddy. All the time."

"They loved each other a lot."

"It's not fair!"

"It sure isn't," she agrees. "But you must understand, you mother needs to be with men again."

"She does not!"

"Certainly, she does. As a matter of fact, there's a lovely fellow I've been meaning to invite to dinner all week. An associate of my stockbroker," she adds, "very successful. . . ."

I've heard enough! With a jolt, I pull the covers over my head, plugging up my ears and ducking toward the foot of the bed. Stockbroker, phooey.

For the first time in nearly a year, I dream about my father. There he is, as clear as day, to touch and talk to. The deep easy tones of his voice are familiar, unclouded. We are jogging in my dream. Just the two of us.

"You're sure I'm not too old for this?" he jokes as we begin our second lap around the Reservoir.

"No complaints, Daddy! We need to keep in shape."

"Okay, okay." He surrenders reluctantly.

That's when I spot the camera bulging under his bold yellow sweatshirt. What a sneak! I might have guessed he'd pull something like this.

"How could you!" I wail. "This is supposed to be *our* time, Daddy."

"I have to bring it."

"You do not," I insist, wondering if he's going to spot that sheep dog on the corner, the one with the big red bow on one ear.

"When that picture is there," he explains patiently, his eyes fixed on the dog, "you've got to seize the moment. Or you lose it, forever. . . ."

I sit up straight. "Where is he?" I yell into the night.

Then Gram is leaning over the side of my bed. The

thinnest slice of autumn moon peeks through our window to light up her face. She smooths my hair, fluffs the pillows.

"You were dreaming," she croons. "Go to sleep, my Pete, go to sleep."

The next morning, Saturday, Mom and I bump into Mr. Rosenblume in the quiet of our lobby. What a sight he is! Those faded blue sweatpants bag around his knees and the funny knit ski band that's been dropping stitches since last winter manages to cover the tips of his ears, but just barely. Sweat drips down the side of his bristly face. His arms are crisscrossed over chest, very casual, probably to hide the big wet splotches underneath.

"Hello!" He smiles at Mom, but doesn't even look at me. "You missed a great sunrise, Ellen."

"My fault." I step between them. "All my sweatshirts are in the wash and it took ten minutes to track down my right sneaker."

I walk toward the door to try to get us away from Mr. Rosenblume, but Mom lingers, leaning against the marbled wall to retie her shoelace. Her keys slip to the floor, and he quickly reaches for them. A brown mitten drops out of her pocket and he picks that up too, handing it to her just as their eyes seem to lock.

"Come on, Mom!" I pull her away by the crook of her arm.

"Okay, boss." She winks, then waves to Mr. Rosenblume, "See you around, Henry."

But Henry follows her out the door, practically stepping on her heels while he's at it. "Going up to the Reservoir?" he asks.

"Mom says it's too far."

She makes a face at me. "I used to run up there a lot," she brags, "but these days, who's got time . . . ?"

"You've got to *make* time." He yanks off the ski band. When he shakes out his head, the tight black curlicues don't even budge. Mom is right. Mr. Rosenblume is handsome. "Those views," he goes on, "they're too good to pass up."

"I remember." Mom pulls on the worn woolen mittens, then hooks her elbow into mine. "*Ciao,* Henry."

"Tomorrow!" He snaps two fingers in the air. "Why didn't I think of it sooner?"

"Tomorrow?"

"We'll all run up to the Reservoir at six o'clock!" He says it like he's suggesting a weekend in Paris.

"Great," I say flatly, wondering if I will pass out or just plain die before we get halfway around. Besides, where's the big thrill for Mr. Rosenblume? He's the one who jogs up there all the time.

"Do I look like some kind of jock?" Mom is giggling. "Six o'clock on a Sunday morning is obscene! You must admit, Henry, you've gotten kind of fanatical in the last couple of years."

"Okay, okay." His hand juts forward in a compromising gesture. "We'll meet down in the lobby at seven."

I know Henry better than anyone, Lily had said, *and he is smitten*. Even though I tried to laugh off the possibility at the time, I wonder now if Lily was right. Maybe her father is beginning to like Mom. And from the look on my mother's face, I wouldn't exactly say she hates the sight of him either.

"My mother needs her beauty sleep on Sunday mornings," I tell Mr. Rosenblume. "We'll have to skip it. . . ."

"Pete!" Mom interrupts. "We certainly won't skip it. I think running the Reservoir is a splendid idea."

I bite my lower lip and glare at Mr. Rosenblume.

"I wish Lily would do a little more in the exercise department," he is saying. "She's so lazy!"

Mom disagrees. "Not Lily. She's anything but lazy. Those wheels are turning," she insists, pointing to the side of her head. "They are turning."

Mr. Rosenblume shrugs. "Well then, I will see the two of you at seven." He rubs the face of his watch, then holds it up to his ear. "Don't be late!"

"He sure is excited about a jog he takes every day of his life," I mutter when Mom and I are trotting down the ramp into the park.

"Mm-hmm." She stops at her favorite warming-up tree.

"Gram says Lily's mother is an idiot for leaving Mr. Rosenblume."

"Your grandmother is very opinionated." Mom clicks her tongue in disapproval.

"Well, do you think it's fair to walk out on your family the way she did?"

"Fair!" Mom's eyes are flashing. "There is no such

thing; you already know that, Pete." Her tone is bitter. "Your own father is dead—a heart attack one minute and dead the next. Is that supposed to be fair?"

Her outburst is so sudden and unexpected that I take a step backwards, as if she had slapped my face. In the same instant, I feel my eyes well up and I want to reach out and hug her, to keep her from hurting anymore.

"Remember, there are at least two sides to the Rosenblumes' story," she goes on with a composed little shudder. "People like Gram, who tend to see the world in black and white, forget all about the shades of gray in between."

"What do you mean?"

"The shades of gray," she says, "where nobody is right or wrong. Sometimes, Pete, there is no right or wrong."

As we start running on the winding park road, I ask, "Do you think her parents will get back together, like Lily said that day?"

"I doubt it," she answers. "But how can you blame a twelve-year-old for looking for the happy ending . . . ?"

"Don't you believe in happy endings anymore?"

Mom flinches in surprise, as if I've just touched a raw nerve. She doesn't answer my question, but there's something about her sad expression that tells me she's thinking about my father again. And one thing is certain. No matter what Gram says about matchmaking and no matter what Lily says about her father's latest crush, my mother just isn't ready to go out with men.

CHAPTER

6

"So then he said we should meet in the morning for a run around the Reservoir." I am trying to keep the edge out of my voice.

"You've got to be kidding!"

"My mother couldn't say yes fast enough," I complain.

Stretched across her unmade bed, we are whiling away the early afternoon. A shrinking pile of peanut butter-and-jelly sandwiches is wedged between us and loose sheets of notebook paper mark a trail of unfinished homework all around.

Lily takes a slug of soda from the green plastic bottle, then passes it to me. "You and I will just have to keep an eye on them," she says thoughtfully, "so things don't get out of hand."

"Keep an eye on them?"

"To make sure everything stays *friendly*, if you know what I mean." Lily peels the crust off her sandwich and pushes it, inch by inch, into her mouth. "Let's call it a little A.R.M."

"What's A.R.M.?"

"Anti-Romance Mission."

"Romance!" I snort. "Aren't you rushing things, Lily?"

She shakes her head knowingly. "He *is* single, available, and handsome. Your own mother even said so. She's single, available, and pretty attractive herself. Now, put two and two together. What do you get?"

"Romance." I gulp solemnly.

Suddenly Lily's toes reach for the ceiling, and she swings both legs in a wide arc, down over the side of the bed. She balances on one foot to inspect her over-stuffed closet, reminding me just now of those girls in *Seventeen*. Probably it's the lacy white camisole, or those black-glitter tights. And once again I realize it's only a matter of time until the boys find her. Roger Starr is just the beginning. Lucky Lily.

Impatient, she tugs a long denim skirt from its hanger, then slips it over her head. When she buttons the waistband, it drops inches toward her skinny hips.

"Don't you love this?" She twirls twice. "My mom loaned it to me last summer. High-style ranch wear," she adds, sounding for a moment just like her mother.

Next she pulls a pair of boots, dusty and with pointed toes, from underneath the bed. I can tell by the biggish look of them they must be her mother's too.

"My father gave Nina the old heave-ho last night," she reports as she wraps a lime-green sash around her waist.

"Uh oh." I can't help giggling. "One more broken heart in the Big Apple."

"She had it coming," Lily says agreeably. "Too pushy."

"And how would you know?"

"Just paying attention." She grins sheepishly. "And listening for the signals."

"You call it signals. I call it minding other people's business."

"If I don't watch him, how am I supposed to understand why Henry does the things he does?"

"You aren't his psychiatrist, just his kid, Lily! He's not supposed to tell you about . . . about . . . certain things."

"You can say it, Pete." She starts walking toward me, very slowly. "*Sex,*" she whispers into my ear, arching those curvy black eyebrows. "*Sex!*"

Blushing disease. Here it comes, the warm flush scooting all the way up to my hairline, then down to my fingertips. Lily says it's a childhood thing. She says it goes away the day you start accepting the facts of life, but I'm not so sure.

She, on the other hand, is perfectly at ease reporting her father's girl friend slept over. Or didn't sleep over. Or nearly slept over. I marvel that we have grown up practically in one house and she's the one who turned out so wise.

Once in a while though, I have to wonder if maybe she's exaggerating one or two of these stories. How is it possible for Mr. Rosenblume to have so many girl friends? I doubt there's a whole lot of time left over after working all day and then taking care of two kids. Anyway, why would he even want so many pushy ladies in his life?

"Roger's coming over this afternoon." Lily's tone is casual.

"Again?" I'm panicked. "When?"

"Any minute." She takes a look at her watch. Calm! How can she be so calm? "He wants me to hear his new Springsteen album."

"You already heard it," I remind her snippily. "Last Sunday when he came over."

Lily grins. "Maybe I want to hear it again."

"Well, maybe *I* better get out of here," I say, leaping off the bed.

"Oh, Pete. I wasn't planning to sleep with him." She says that just to watch my face turn red, I know it. "Stick around," she urges. "Roger said he might bring Jon along this time."

"Stick around? After the way my mother bawled him out the other morning, I haven't got the nerve to be in the same room as Jon Hill!"

"He's probably forgotten all about it. Anyway," she warns, "boys that cute are hard to come by."

"He *is* cute," I admit with a sigh.

But a minute later the doorbell rings and I am flying past Lily, through the kitchen and onto the service elevator, then into my bedroom where I crawl under the covers. Maybe forever.

"Wake up, Pete." The voice is hushed, and I smell her coffee even before my eyes blink open.

"What time is it?" I groan.

"Nearly seven." Mom sits cross-legged at the foot of my bed. She sips from that silly ceramic mug I made my father in second grade. He used to carry it from room to room as he shaved and showered and dressed for work. "Did you forget?" Mom is saying. "We're going up to the Reservoir, with Henry."

"How could I forget?" I fumble in a bottom drawer for long flowery underwear, then start pulling the skin-tight stuff on.

Across the gray-light room, Gram sits up in her bed. "Good morning!" she sings, punching up the pillows behind her.

"You stay put," Mom orders cheerfully. "I will bring a treat."

"*She's* perky enough," Gram mumbles, dropping a row of pink rollers across the width of her lap.

Mom reappears juggling a tall glass of orange juice in one hand and a steaming coffee in the other. The Sunday papers are crammed under her elbow. Dumping the bulk of newspaper on Gram's bed, she says, "This ought to keep you busy until Pete and I get back."

"Did you say you're jogging with Henry? Henry Rosenblume?" Gram pulls apart the fat sections.

"That's right."

Gram runs her finger down a long column of numbers. "You'll enjoy spending a little time with a man," she says, without taking her eyes off the page.

"See you later, Mother." Mom turns on her heels and heads out of the room.

47

"What did I tell you, Pete!" Gram whispers excitedly. "She *is* ready. . . ."

"Gram!" I scold, tying a fat green ribbon around my unruly ponytail. "Leave my mother alone. . . ."

"It's seven o'clock!" Mom is calling from the front foyer. "Shake a leg, Pete."

I gulp down half a glass of juice. "Here goes nothing."

"I'll fix a nice breakfast," Gram promises cheerfully. "Pancakes, to revive you."

I finish tying up my sneakers in the elevator. "Gram sure has a one-track mind," I tell my mother. "All she thinks about— Wait a minute! Are you wearing lipstick, Mom, at seven o'clock in the morning?"

"Must be the shadows." She points to the dim yellow bulb overhead.

Shadows nothing! It *is* lipstick, and there's only one reason she would be wearing it. To impress . . .

The elevator creaks to a stop on two. Mr. Rosenblume steps in. Lily steps in behind him. She is wearing a chic new sweatshirt with holes in one elbow and a circle of rhinestones near the neck.

"See what a little preaching will do." Mr. Rosenblume's tone is playful. "I finally managed to embarrass Lily into coming along."

I don't dare look at Lily. It's pretty clear her father doesn't know the *real* reason she's coming along. The real reason is that we're going to get a head start on our Anti-Romance Mission. It is urgent to keep an eye on our parents.

The entrance to the park is just a couple of blocks

away, but today it seems like twenty. It's weird the way the four of us are acting like a bunch of strangers. Mom and I walk a few steps behind Lily and her father. Nobody talks and I want to go home but can't think of a proper excuse. Stomachache? Too tired? Tendonitis?

"Try these toe-touches, to stretch out the spine." Mr. Rosenblume hangs upside down over a patch of brown grass just inside the park. "Easy, slow stretches . . ."

"I hate sit-ups," Mom groans a few minutes later, when Mr. Rosenblume orders us to try thirty with knees bent. The hard kind.

"Warming up is essential," he says unsympathetically. "Lily! Pete! Ellen! Let's tone up those stomach muscles. . . ."

"Ugh!"

Finally we are heading up to Eighty-sixth Street on pretty tree-lined roads. A pack of cyclists whizzes past in single file, almost as one. Leaning forward on skinny handlebars, they are flashy and handsome in black stretch shorts, bold multicolored shirts, and those neat little racing caps that flap up in front.

"Keep it clean, Jellybean!" Lily calls to a cute redhead as he speeds by. He turns around and smiles at her.

By the time we get to the Reservoir, I'm ready to call it quits. "Are you up to this?" I whisper to Lily. "It's a mile and a half around!"

"Of course I am." She rolls her eyes. "You know what a great athlete I am."

"Wait for us!" I yell to Mom and Mr. Rosenblume,

who already started around the Reservoir. The dirt path is narrow, so even if Lily and I could catch up, which we couldn't, it would be impossible to run alongside them. "Physical fitness maniacs," I grumble.

"Move it, girls!" A little man in yellow long johns scoots between us, and I nearly fall into the row of prickly hedges.

"Road hog," Lily hisses.

I can't take my eyes off Mom and Mr. Rosenblume. Yards ahead, they are jogging and talking and talking and jogging. Granted, she's a good enough runner, being a mother and all. This morning, though, her feet are flying out behind her! Also, she is laughing like crazy, and I'd like to know what's so darned funny.

"What's so funny?" Lily mutters, echoing my thoughts.

"I had no idea your father was such a comedian," I answer sarcastically.

"He's not," she says knowingly. "They're just giggling. I'll tell you one thing, though. There's *definitely* a touch of chemistry in the air."

"If your father's looking for chemistry, he better look somewhere else," I grump, tugging at loose red sweatpants. "My mom isn't available."

"And a new love affair for Henry is entirely out of the question."

Out of breath, we stop and lean against the high wire fence that surrounds the Reservoir. My jagged West Side skyline is reflected in the choppy water, those old-time buildings wriggling a bit in the morning breeze.

Lily pulls two sheets of paper from underneath her turtleneck. No doubt another letter from her mother, the only person I know who writes on lavender paper with lines across. Probably she imports it from Bloomingdale's too.

Lily starts to read. "'Christmas in New York is magic. I feel worse than ever at holiday time, and the mother in me longs to jump on the next plane home. A family again, but a happy one this time . . . '"

I tune out. *A family again . . . a family again . . .* the words are floating around my head. Me too! I want to be a family again. . . .

"Are you paying attention?" Lily shakes the letter in front of my face. "My mother's miserable, Pete. She wants to come home."

"But what about The Cowboy?" I ask as we start running.

"My mother wants us to be a family again," Lily says, sounding oddly childish. She stuffs the letter back in her shirt. "The Cowboy can stay in Wyoming. Where he belongs."

As we struggle past an ancient wrinkled lady in hot pink running shoes, the sun is just breaking out of thick morning clouds to trim the treetops all around. I hear my feet clumping against the damp soil, but right now they feel as if they belong to someone else. If only they did!

Far ahead of us, Mom and Henry Rosenblume are rounding the last bend. As they slow down and finally stop running, he has the nerve—and I mean nerve—to

51

put his arm around her shoulder! It's only for a second that he keeps it there, but there's no changing the fact that he did it.

Now I've seen everything.

So has Lily. "A.R.M.," she spells quietly and deliberately.

"Anti-Romance Mission," I say, putting my hand on her shoulder, glad at least we are in on this together. "But how are we going to keep up with them if we're such lousy runners?"

"We'll just have to get in better shape," she answers. "You stick with me, kiddo. We'll be doing eight–minute miles in no time!"

"Oh sure!" I say, laughing out loud.

But when I turn to look at her, somehow I have the feeling she means business. With a capital *B*.

CHAPTER

7

On Monday, Lily stays home with "a touch of flu." She blames it on yesterday's heavy dose of exercise. I think she's a hypochondriac. After school I rap on her front door to she if she's recovered. A few minutes later, white as a ghost, she pulls it open. Lifting an arm in a halfhearted wave, she pivots on barefoot heels. I follow her back to bed.

"Slow death," she moans as I tuck the puffy quilt all around her. Her long black hair is moist, matted down, and miserably tangled.

"You look awful," I say sympathetically, putting my hand on her forehead. "You even have temperature, Lily! Where's Jake?"

"Your grandmother took him upstairs. She's been in and out all day," Lily adds wanly, "a regular Florence Nightingale."

"Our Anti-Romance Mission won't survive the week without you, so you better pull yourself together." I stoop to pick up a dirty nightgown and three un-matched knee socks. "This place is a wreck!"

"I'm sick, Pete. No lectures!"

I sit beside her pouring ginger ale from the glass bottle on the floor beside her bed. "Drink this," I suggest kindly. "It's supposed to help."

"Did you happen, by any chance, to see Roger to-day?" she asks, perking up a notch.

"Once, in the cafeteria," I answer, pulling three sticks of bubble gum from my back pocket.

"And you told him I'm extremely ill, maybe terminal?"

"I told him never to come to your house again. I told him it's a good thing he didn't bring Jon Hill along on Saturday. I told him you hate his precious Springsteen. And I told him he gave you the flu and who knows what else."

Lily giggles weakly. "Now tell me what *really* happened."

"You know I never said boo to Roger Starr!" I ex-claim.

"Will you ever learn, kiddo, boys don't bite!"

I push all three pieces of gum into my mouth. "You're a real wise guy, Lily, especially for someone on her deathbed."

But she isn't paying attention. "Don't leave," she whispers as her heavy eyelids flutter, droop, and close.

I blow out a big pink bubble. "Best friends don't desert each other in hard times," I assure her.

This time she doesn't answer. She is fast asleep.

I find Jake upstairs in 9B. He is crawling along the kitchen floor making siren noises and pushing a red fire engine around Gram's ankles. She doesn't seem to notice though, she's so busy maneuvering pots across the top of the stove.

"Looks like you're cooking up a storm," I say.

"We're having company." Gram hands me a carrot stick.

"Who?"

"Alan Lipshitz."

"Who's he?"

"You'll see later, Pete."

As she groups yellow tulips in a thin glass vase, I can't help noticing how fancy the table looks tonight. There's the ugly striped tablecloth, instead of our nice straw mats, and cloth napkins with fringe, instead of the usual paper ones. Wineglasses too! This is beginning to look suspicious.

"Does Mom know he's coming?"

"Not yet."

"Are you *matchmaking* or something?" I am trying to keep the panic out of my voice.

Gram ignores my question. But I'm clever enough to figure out Alan Lipshitz is coming to my house for a *reason*.

I take Jake home and put him in a bath with bubbles. He soaks for an hour with two plastic hydrofoils and a flotilla of sailboats, three naked soldiers, and an orange submarine. Afterward he decides on the green frog pajamas with feet, and he follows me to the kitchen.

"What do you want for supper?" I ask, towel-drying his hair. "I'm in charge until your father gets home."

"Hamburger and ketchup. Let's play you're the mommy!"

I peel stubborn foil from a frozen patty and dump it into the heavy cast-iron pan. It sizzles noisily and smokes. Cooking is not my favorite part of this game. But when Jake drags a chair clear across the room to stand as tall as me, one little arm draped around my waist, I *know* playing mommy has some good moments too. I kiss his cheek, spotty with freckles, and he wipes it away with a smile.

Half an hour later he has eaten one—possibly two— bites. Mostly, though, he tracks the partially cooked hamburger through squiggly trails of ketchup. It looks disgusting, and I tell him so. I am scrubbing impatiently at the smelly grease-pan when the front door clicks open.

Jake flies into his father's arms.

"How's Lily?" Mr. Rosenblume, hugging Jake, pulls his eyebrows toward each other in that worried-parent way.

"She's asleep." I toss the scroungy soap pad into the garbage. "I better get home now. We're having company."

"Who's that?" Mr. Rosenblume looks curious. He slips off his tie and hangs it on the handle of the refrigerator door.

"I have a feeling he's one of those *eligible bachelors* Gram wants my mom to meet. If you ask me," I continue, lowering my voice, "Gram's making a big mistake."

"Mistake?"

"My mother's not a bit interested in meeting men!"

"Really?" Mr. Rosenblume looks surprised.

"She misses my father too much," I explain, looking him straight in the eye and remembering how he put his arm around Mom's shoulder yesterday morning. "Nobody could replace *him*," I add to make my point crystal-clear.

"Of course."

"Anyway, you're right about the Reservoir. It is pretty!"

"We'll go again." Now he is looking *me* straight in the eye.

And what is that supposed to mean? We'll all go again—he and Mom, Lily and I? Or, is he trying to tell me something else, that he wants to go alone with Mom next time? Impossible! My mother jogs with me. Or she jogs alone, before work. What she doesn't do is jog with men. Period.

I am glaring at the clock on the kitchen wall. The hands won't budge. 7:07. Tonight there are four of us sitting at the kitchen table. Mom isn't talking. I talk but only when someone makes me. Gram is chattering away. And Alan Lipshitz couldn't be creepier if he tried.

"So you're the publishing tycoon!" He smiles at Mom. His voice is so loud he seems to be yelling at her.

57

"I just work at the magazine. *Employee*," she responds coolly, spitting out each syllable.

He smiles again.

"There's a piece of broccoli in your teeth," I tell him politely.

Mom rolls her eyes, trying not to laugh. Then she goes back to stabbing at the colorful vegetable casserole Gram spent half the day preparing.

"Alan is such a brilliant stockbroker," Gram is saying, trying to ignore Mom and me.

"We have mint dental floss in the medicine cabinet," I say to no one in particular.

"And how old are you, Patricia?" shouts Alan Lipshitz.

"What?"

"Alan asked how old you are." Gram is angry.

"I'm twelve and nobody calls me Patricia. I'm Pete. *P-e-t-e*." I guess I don't need to be quite this rude, but somehow I feel terrific!

He turns to Mom and tries again. "I like your apartment, Ellen. A little cramped, I guess, but fine city views."

Mom looks up from her plate with green-ice eyes. I can't tell if she's going to punch him in the nose or pour a glass of red wine on his perfect coiffed head. She doesn't do either though. What a shame!

"Do you have any kids?" I ask sweetly.

"Kids?" He yanks at his starched collar. "Oh, no!"

"Don't you *like* kids, Mr. Lipshitz?"

"Enough, Pete!" Gram is furious.

At nine thirty our esteemed visitor kisses Gram's cheek, shakes Mom's hand, puffs his brown cigar at me, then heads across town to his penthouse with two skylights. Good riddance!

"How could you do it?" Mom bellows at Gram the minute he is out the door. "You didn't even warn me he was coming."

"Lovely man." Gram calmly slips dishes into the sink.

"He is twenty pounds overweight. He's got bad breath, prissy table manners, and he loves himself to distraction!" Mom cries.

"He was quite taken with *you*, Ellen. I could tell in a minute."

"How could you tell, Gram?" I can't help asking.

For the next ten minutes Mom flaps around the kitchen banging silverware into a drawer and flinging fringed napkins across the table. She opens and closes cabinets without taking anything out or putting anything in. Finally she whirls around to confront Gram.

"N.I. *No Interest*," she says between clenched teeth. "And you've got to stop interfering, Mother!"

Next thing I know Gram is packing up.

"I'm only trying to make her life a little nicer," she explains as I watch her fold cashmere sweaters into a pile on my bed.

Mom comes into the room. "Don't leave," she says stiffly.

"I'm going back to Miami."

"Stay." Mom sighs. "We need you."

Gram breaks into a smile. "All right. I will stay, but just for a while."

"And no more funny business," Mom warns, narrowing her eyes at Gram.

"No more funny business." Gram is solemn.

"I will find my own boyfriends," Mom says quietly.

"You will?" I gulp. "But Mom . . ."

"Like I said," Mom cuts in, "I will date *whom* I please, when I please." She stands at the window, her back to us. "Do you both understand what I'm saying?"

"Of course," Gram answers quickly.

But I don't say anything. *I will find my own boyfriends.* Surely Mom couldn't mean it. She couldn't be ready to forget all about my father. She couldn't be ready for men in her life.

Not yet.

CHAPTER

8

Morning already?

The little red clock shrieks in my ear. I jam it under the pillow. 5:50. This is madness! I count to ten. I take a couple of slow, deep breaths. I muster just enough energy to hang two heavy legs over the side of the bed.

"I think I hate you," I tell Lily in the quiet of the lobby.

"Impossible, kiddo." She snaps up her father's red ski vest.

Our Anti-Romance Mission is off to a running start. Now that she's recovered from her mystery flu, Lily is more determined than ever to get us in shape. She studies the running manuals to compare the wisdom of the experts. Reading aloud as we walk to and from school, she stuffs her knapsack and mine with free brochures from Upper West Side sport shops. On Sunday, she made me sit through the most boring lecture in the world at the YMCA: *Running for a Longer Life*. She even thinks we're on some weirdo high protein diet. All this so we can trail our parents in Central Park!

On Monday, Tuesday, and Friday mornings we're scheduled to meet downstairs at six. Sharp. Since we aren't allowed in the park before sunrise, these early morning jogs are restricted to Central Park West, between Sixty-fourth and Seventy-seventh Streets. Twenty city blocks make a mile and each day we add one block to our distance. Lily, also known as Coach, plots the course. Which amounts to deciding if we head north first, or south. She keeps a clipboard under the leather armchair in the lobby, with graph paper and rows of numbers, to monitor our progress. Sometimes she brings down her father's silvery timepiece.

Today is cold and wet. Miserable in the extreme.

"You'll catch flu again," I grumble, "and so will I!"

"How come you don't carry on like this when you jog with your mother?" Lily bends to roll up those great leg warmers from Bendel's, the argyle ones in shades of pink. They remind me of strawberry ice-cream sodas.

"I'm just looking out for your health," I answer, pulling on purple earmuffs. The dollar-a-pair kind from an illegal midtown pushcart.

"Today we'll run up to the Museum of Natural History, for starters," Lily informs me. "So, watch out for cracks in the sidewalk, open stairwells, potholes, and uneven curbs. And traffic, Pete. Watch out for traffic."

"Right, Coach."

Lily hates warming up as much as I do, so we agreed

to do it only once a week. This is not a warm-up day. I squint against the tickle-rain and start a slow run.

"Morning, Handsome!" Lily waves to the doorman standing outside Number 101. Surprised, he stops his yawning and stretching to grin at her and whistle.

"You are the biggest flirt this side of the Hudson River!" I tell her, wishing I had the nerve to do it too.

"Talk about flirting," Lily answers in her big-sister tone of voice, "Roger and Jon are meeting us at The Ice Cream Boutique on Friday afternoon. I found out Jon loves ice cream as much as you do," she adds enthusiastically.

"Friday is no good for me," I lie, "and I think I'm on a diet."

"I'm only trying to make your life a little nicer."

"Well, maybe you and my grandmother ought to go into the matchmaking business," I suggest, "since you're both so good at it."

Lily laughs. "You're scared to death," she says knowingly. "But you'll get over it, Pete. After all, they're only boys."

"Only boys!" I repeat with a snort. "How can you be so cool?"

"To think that you and I may soon be going steady with the cutest and second cutest boy in school . . ." She whistles dreamily.

At Seventy-seventh Street we make wide arcs, then continue running downtown. Yanking her father's stopwatch from her pocket, she frowns. "I'm ashamed to log this on my clipboard. We're moving like two old cows today, Pete."

"A kind syllable once in a while wouldn't be the worst thing in the world." I exhale a mouthful of stale air. My feet are dragging behind me.

"Potassium's what you need. And more Vitamin D."

"Praise and admiration, that's what I need. And by the way, Coach, count me out on Friday. I'm in no mood for a rendezvous with Jon Hill."

She pretends not to hear me. "How about another quarter mile this morning?" she suggests as we make our final U-turns on Sixty-fourth Street.

"Impossible!" I groan.

"You've got to *push*," she insists, looking pretty exhausted herself.

"I can't!" Breathing hard and panting noisily, I rest a palm flat against my chest. "This can't be good for me," I add, feeling sorry for myself.

All of a sudden she grabs my sleeve and pulls me to the ground. We squat behind a red car parked in front of our building. Lily's eyes are wide open and so is her mouth.

"There they go!" she whispers, waving a fist at me. I look up to see her father and my mother jogging down the street.

"But it's Tuesday." I peek around the chrome fender. "Mom never runs on Tuesday. That's the day they always have editorial meetings. . . ."

"They planned it." Lily's tone is menacing.

"Coincidence." My tone is doubtful.

"It is 6:28 on a Tuesday morning and you call this a coincidence?"

"Lily."

"What?"

"I think we better trail them."

We follow them to the park. There are obstacles every step of the way, but nothing can stop us. We need to stay far enough behind so Mom and Mr. Rosenblume don't know we're here, but it's still so dark we could easily lose sight of them! Not to mention the overall creepy feeling I have from sneaking around Central Park in the pitch-blackness. Besides, I'm tired. We've already run two miles this morning. . . .

We surge ahead though, and manage to keep perfect trailing distance. For a while, anyway. But of course those two have all the energy in the world, and they sprint along the darkened road. I plod half a stride behind Lily, wondering how I'm going to make it down to Fifty-ninth Street, let alone all the way around . . . or maybe they're planning a private little side trip to the Reservoir. . . .

"You're fading, kiddo." Lily reaches for my arm. "Try and stick with it.

But it's hopeless. At the beginning of the lower loop, I haul myself, like a doubled-over sack of potatoes, onto the side of the road.

"Sorry," I apologize between wheezy old-lady breaths.

"There's always next time." Lily keeps her eyes fixed on the shrinking outline of our parents. "And one thing is certain," she adds grimly. "There *will* be a next time."

CHAPTER
9

On Friday Lily and I get caught in a rainstorm on our way home from school. But we are armed against the elements in slickers and rubber boots, and we dawdle, as usual, on one avenue or another.

"There's no way Roger and Jon what's-his-name will be at The Ice Cream Boutique." Tilting my nose to the bleak afternoon sky, I giggle when the raw shower sprays my face. "Boys hate getting wet."

"We'll see about that," Lily answers.

At Seventy-fifth and Columbus, we stop to browse in Antiques by Annie, where Lily continues her search for a 1920s rainhat. Smug as a fine-arts dealer, she leads me up and down the musty aisles. She says the twenty-watt bulbs give the place atmosphere but I'll take track lighting any day, and I fold my arms in front of me to keep from brushing against the dusty furniture. Golden hangers sway from angled poles on the ceiling, showing off

Annie's antique clothing. To me, it all looks like a bunch of junk.

"Check out this French armoire!" Lily calls, waving from the back corner of the store.

I pull open tall oak doors. They creak and groan. Spotting myself in the full-length mirror, I gasp and take a step backward.

"We can't let Jon see you looking like this," she teases, dropping a big straw hat over my head.

"I already told you, Lily, those guys won't show," I answer with surprising confidence.

Turning on her heel, she heads for the jewelry counter. An ancient glamorous lady with powder-pale skin, red lipstick, and no mascara at all watches us closely.

"How's it going today, Annie?" Lily's tone is friendly as she leans over the counter. "Did you ever sell that checkered turn-of-the-century rainhat?"

"You know who bought it?" Annie chuckles. "A dead ringer for Marilyn Monroe!"

Lily hovers over the glass case studying rows of earrings and charms, bangle bracelets and beady necklaces.

"Pete, I have news," she says quietly and without looking at me. "Henry went out with your mother."

"Out?" I repeat.

"They went to dinner last night." She presses her lips together.

"My mother worked late last night," I hear myself tell her. As we walk out into the storm again, I am glad of the cold wet air to breathe.

We duck under the striped awning of City Sweets. All around, buckets of rain splash to the sidewalk in loud splats. I stare blankly at the trays of crullers and fruit-filled muffins. Tuesday jogging. Thursday dinner date. A *secret* dinner date, no less.

"It's fine with me if your mother starts going out," Lily says. "Only she ought to know better than to go out with Henry! Especially since my mother's coming home. I *told* her, Pete. You heard me. . . ."

"Are you sure about that dinner date?" I cut in.

"I saw the American Express check."

"Maybe he went with someone else," I suggest hopefully.

"They came home in the same cab. I know, because I was watching from the living-room window."

"So much for A.R.M." I sigh. "What good is all our spying anyway?"

"We mustn't give up. *Especially* now."

We leap across shallow pools of muddy water and stop in front of The Ice Cream Boutique.

"No boys!" I sing. A wonderful sense of relief settles over me and I order a mocha-chip cone, double-scoop, from the shivering teenager behind the counter. She flashes me one of those you've-gotta-be-nuts-to-eat-ice-cream-on-a-day-like-this looks.

As I reach into my knapsack for money, someone steps up behind Lily. Someone named Roger Starr. Gently putting two athletic hands over her eyes, he talks into her ear. "Guess who?"

"Paul Newman." Lily glows. So would I if Roger Starr whispered in my ear.

"Guess again." His voice is low-keyed and very sexy. Even though Roger doesn't acknowledge the fact that I'm alive, my knees are getting weaker by the minute.

"Michael Jackson!" Lily taps her fingertips across his bony knuckles.

"Guess right this time and the ice cream's on me."

"Okay, Roger. Your treat!" And she pushes his beautiful strong hands off her face. Whirling around, she dazzles him with those straight white teeth. The rain that makes me look like a soggy old subway rat somehow leaves her looking better than ever! Even her hair shimmers from the downpour, while mine is stringy, ugly and matted down to my head.

Just then I see another kid, a shorter huskier one with grimy Nikes on his feet and gum in his mouth. Jon Hill. Leaning against the skinny green bike that had hooked itself to Mom's sweatshirt, he is totally engrossed in his chocolate ice-cream cone. I zero in on his face. Even though he isn't movie-star handsome the way Roger is, I'm convinced already that Lily's right. Jon certainly is the second cutest boy in P.S.7. No doubt about it. He's got brown layered hair that needs cutting, pale blue eyes that won't look at me, and a splash of freckles—the small, sweet understated kind.

"Let's go," I croak at Lily.

"Wait." She holds my elbow firmly. "Roger, here's Pete. Pete, this is Jon Hill."

"Hi."

"Hello." That's me, and I'm talking to my toes.

"So how do you like riding around in this monsoon?" Lily kids with Jon. I feel like a bump on a log.

When Jon wipes his mouth with the sleeve of his football jersey, I can't help noticing the way it clings to his body. "It's okay," he says, trying to smile.

"Jon and I are taking a cross-country bike trip next summer," Roger boasts, stepping closer to Lily. "Rain will be the least of our problems."

All of a sudden Lily's inviting them to walk us home. I try to signal her with my eyes, to let her know what a rotten idea this is, but it's too late. Roger follows her out to Seventy-second Street and walks alongside her, holding his book bag alternately over her head and his. They're gabbing away and laughing at their own jokes, and I can't hear a word of it.

Jon wheels his bike parallel to me but about two yards away, like I have bubonic plague or something. I pretend not to notice. I pretend to enjoy the drizzle and our dead silence.

To make matters worse, Lily has the nerve to invite them upstairs! I want to go home in the worst way, but then I remember about Mom and her secret dinner date with Henry Rosenblume, and I feel angry and not ready to confront her.

Lily's apartment is dark and quiet. No Mr. Rosenblume. Not even Jake and the baby-sitter. My stomach is doing back flips and somersaults. I am miserable.

Lily pulls her new Springsteen from the stack of records. She bought it Wednesday, probably to impress Roger Starr. Standing at the living-room window, she moves shoulders and hips to the beat of the music. Roger stretches across the couch to tell her something. It must be pretty funny because she throws her head back and laughs with glee. What did I come here for?

Jon manages to look as uncomfortable as I feel. He walks around the room, stooping every so often to examine one of Jake's cars or trucks. Once he even tries to talk to me.

"How is your mother's sweatshirt?" he asks. "Did she need a patch or anything?"

"No problem," I assure him, pushing Jake's tiny Coke truck along the edge of the bookshelf. I imagine myself looping an arm around Jon's waist and pulling him close for a kiss or two. *Did you know you're the second cutest kid in school,* I would say. And I would flash him the sexiest kind of half smile. And he would say, *You're not so bad yourself.*

I hide out in the bathroom awhile, studying myself in the mirror and wishing I could be beautiful or even in the very pretty category. I try pulling a comb through my hair, but it's full of wet knots. Finally I tie it back with a soggy ribbon from my pocket.

I slide open the medicine cabinet to inspect. Aspirin, iodine, Band-Aids, Vaseline, cotton swabs, black eyeliner, and the purple mascara from Woolworth's. . . .

"Pete!" Lily flings open the bathroom door just as I finish doing my left eye. "You're acting like a baby!"

"I am not."

"Well, come out of there. Roger and Jon are leaving and want to say good-bye."

"They needn't bother!" I hiss. "They're ignoring me anyway!"

"That's not true. I saw Jon talk to you."

I make a face. "And I saw Roger whispering in your ear like there's no tomorrow!"

"I like it when he does that," she answers with a sly little smile. "Now would you come out of here?"

"All right," I grumble, reaching for the doorknob. "But I wish you'd quit trying to fix me up with Jon Hill. He's way too shy."

Lily laughs. "I think what you need is more practice."

"At the rate I'm going," I say, flicking off the bathroom light, "I'll need about seven years of practice before I can even look a boy in the eye."

After dinner I find Mom sitting like some yoga enthusiast in the middle of her too-big bed. Surrounded by a thick mess of manuscript pages and magazine layouts, she flips sheets, sips diet soda, jots down notes, and snacks from the bag of pretzels.

I clear my throat.

"Don't squish page eight," she says absently as I move paper to squeeze beside her.

I fidget with the cuff of my blue flannel pajamas, pulling at a strand of thread and watching the hem unravel inch by inch.

"Homework finished, Pete?"

"Mmhmm." I am staring at my father's prize photo—a fat slit-eyed cat hurling himself off a barrel.

"No math problems for me to solve?" She smiles. "Whew!"

"So, Mom. Working late again this week?"

"No." She pops a pretzel stick into her mouth and one into mine. "Why?"

"Just wondering." I loop the curling pajama thread many times around my pinky. "Feeling pretty good these days?"

She looks up. "Yes. I'm fine."

I clear my throat again. "Been to any good restaurants lately?"

When she pushes her glasses back to rest on top of her head, I notice the way her ears stick out a touch more than they should. "Is there something you want to talk about, Pete?"

I look down at my chipped fingernails. What now? Am I supposed to bring up Henry Rosenblume and the dinner date? Me? But I'm only twelve! If only I'd talked over some details with Lily first, she'd know what to say. After all, she's the expert in the department of grown-up affairs . . . but of course she was too busy with Roger to worry about me and my problems. . . .

"Lily thinks you're ready to date," I blurt out.

"She does?" Mom looks surprised. "Well, have you told her about my wonderful date with Alan Lipshitz?"

"Alan Lipshitz?" I repeat, wondering if Mom is just trying to change the subject.

73

Then she says, "He was the drippiest man I've ever met!"

"A real loser." I begin to laugh. "But Gram sure thinks he's the cat's pajamas."

"Correction." Mom points a finger in the air. "I think Alan Lipshitz is more like the cat's long underwear. Last year's long underwear. I was half expecting something like this," she says with a sigh.

"You were?"

"It's always been Gram's way, to try to make me happy. I understand, because I'm a mother too." Mom shrugs. "But she has to learn to mind her own business and let me—let us—find our own way."

"Right."

And she pulls me to her for the biggest kind of hug, the kind that used to come in duplicate, before my father died.

"It's going to take a lot more than some stockbroker to blot the pain of the past year," Mom says softly.

I pull back and search her face for something. She said there was no room for stockbrokers, but she didn't say a thing about Henry Rosenblume. I have about a hundred questions I'd like to ask her, but somehow my nerve is all used up.

CHAPTER

10

Roger Starr is becoming a pain.

The next Friday I am waiting for Lily in the school-yard at three, just like always. Along comes Mr. Beautiful. The first thing I notice is the way his plaid shirt is crammed into tight tan corduroys. Then I focus on black penny loafers and the fact that he's wearing no socks in December. Lily says his eyes are emerald-green, but as he walks toward me I haven't got the courage to check. Then Roger does the most curious thing. He talks to me.

"Hi, Pete. Lily says you should go home without her today." That's it. He hurries away without another word. I'm beginning to hate his guts all right. I wonder why the same boy who can talk up a storm with Lily has nothing to say to me.

Walking home with Lily is an event, even on ordinary days. Walking home alone is a bore. At Seventy-seventh Street I meet a group of girls from school and stand for a moment on the edge of their little clique. But they aren't used to me and make me feel unwelcome. I picture myself strutting past these babyish gigglers, arm in arm with Jon Hill. *She's going steady with Roger Starr's best friend,* they would whisper enviously.

At home I mope around my room awhile, turning lamps on, then turning them off again. I flip pages of Lily's recycled *Seventeen,* thinking about Roger's great face and the way she touched his fingers last Friday, as if she's been touching boys' fingers all her life. I think about me and how I'm never going to be a social butterfly. At five o'clock, when I can't stand my own company another minute, I run down the back stairs to Lily's.

I find her in the bath, up to her chin in bubbles. Her eyes are closed, the black lashes more striking than ever against that white skin. Her hair is piled high on her head and one arm is draped, listless, over the side of the tub.

"Hello, Pete," she croons.

"Where were you after school?" I sit on the edge of the porcelain tub, dragging my hand through the water. "Hanging out with Roger or something?" I try keeping my tone light but somehow I know what's coming.

"Yes."

"You were?" I squeak.

Lily sits up straight. A million bubbles cling to her shoulders. All at once they start popping. One by one and without a sound. "We walked through the park," she reports dreamily. We bought pretzels and a grape soda and we shared it. Then we sat around a deserted playground kicking mud off our shoes."

"What did you guys talk about?" I am trying to take this calmly, really I am, but I feel like I just got punched in the stomach.

"Everything." Lily sighs a deep movie sigh, then dabs both cheeks with white puffs of foam. "I think I'm falling in love." Her eyes are glittering.

Don't say another word, I want to tell her. Instead, I stand abruptly and rub my hands flat against the bathroom mirror, making concentric fog-free circles. My face appears and disappears in the mist. This is what I knew would happen, I remind myself. But why now?

She steps out of the bath wrapped in a big brown towel. When she unclips her fat barrette, Lily's hair falls straight to her shoulders and beyond. She is perfect and I am jealous. With a capital *J*.

"What about Monday?" I demand, following her to the bedroom.

"I'm meeting Roger after school."

"Again?" I stamp my foot.

"Pete, I'm in love," she repeats.

"I'm very glad to hear it," I bark. "And thanks, pal, for two-timing me!"

Lily pulls on a bright red T-shirt. It hangs far below her hips and clings to them. "I'm not two-timing you, Pete."

"*We're* supposed to be best friends!" I shout, heading down the dark hallway to the Rosenblumes' front door.

"We *are* best friends," she calls after me. "But a boy-friend is different."

I find Gram and my mother in the kitchen, huddled over the new Saks catalog. They are unusually easy and relaxed, and I stand just inside the door listening to them.

"This reminds me of your senior prom dress," Gram reminisces. "Remember, Ellen? White satin . . ."

"And that smooth fellow who took me!" Mom chuckles. "I was so sure you put him up to it. Did you, Mother?"

Gram laughs. "I guess I've always tried to interfere a tiny bit, at least where men are concerned."

"A *tiny* bit?"

"Speaking of men," Gram says in a more serious tone, "I was wondering about you and Henry Rosen-blume . . ."

I take three steps into the kitchen and Gram abruptly stops talking. "Hello," I sulk, hoisting myself onto the high stool across from them. "So wouldn't you know, it's finally happened to Lily."

Gram reaches for the platter of sweet-and-sour meat-balls. "What has finally happened?"

"*Boys.*" I lean forward on my elbows. "And one boy in particular."

"Which one?" Mom asks, tossing cherry tomatoes into the salad bowl.

"Roger Starr. He happens to be the cutest, most ador-able boy in the whole entire school," I add miserably.

78

"Lily must like that," Gram notes.

"It's more like *love*," I snort. "They walked home today, and Monday the same."

"And you aren't invited, right, Pete?" One thing about my mother, she sure doesn't beat around the bush.

"I've always known Lily was going to be a knockout." I suck in my breath.

"I know what you mean." Gram marinates meatballs in the sauce pan. "Lily is bright and pretty as a picture. The more she fusses with that makeup, I swear she's the spitting image of her mother. . . ." Her voice trails off. "Yes. The boys will adore her."

"You two sound like Lily's ready to get her own apartment!" Mom jokes.

"There's something else," Gram says. "I think twelve-year-old girls belong with their *mothers*."

Mom gasps in surprise. "Your thinking is pathetically old-fashioned, Mother."

"Lily needs her mother. Full-time," Gram adds firmly.

"Henry Rosenblume," Mom says between clenched teeth, "is every bit the parent a young girl could ask for."

While the two of them hotly debate who would best guide Lily in the affairs of the heart, I realize they aren't even listening to me and my problems! Lily's the one in the pink, not me. She's got Roger Starr. I'm left behind. Like a little kid. Too scared to speak to boys, let alone fall in love with them!

"What about me?" I mutter.

"What about you?"

"Lily's my best friend. Now that she's going around with Mr. Wonderful, what am I supposed to do?"

"You sound pretty selfish." Mom narrows her eyes at me.

Selfish? I'm the one who's losing people right and left. First my father. Then Mom starts having her secret meetings with Henry Rosenblume. And now Lily's positively mushy over Roger. And she says I'm selfish! How come nobody understands?

"You and Lily have been as close as sisters since you were babies." Mom rolls a paper napkin around her forefinger. "There's a very special bond between you."

"Bond or not, Lily won't have time for both of us," I say quietly. "She'll have to choose. Me or Roger."

"No, Pete. We have to make room in our lives for new friends, nobody ever replaces the old ones. They're in our hearts," she adds thoughtfully, "for keeps."

"Lily says a boyfriend is different."

"A boyfriend *is* different. But there is room for both kinds of friends." Mom smiles. "Lily's not the only one who's going to have a boyfriend. One day you will too."

"Not me."

But I think about Jon's drenched football jersey, and the way he rode over to The Ice Cream Boutique in that storm. Most boys would complain like crazy about that sort of thing. So isn't it funny? Jon and I have two things in common already. Ice cream and hanging out in the rain.

Too bad I'll never have the nerve to tell him.

CHAPTER

11

We are flying through Bloomingdale's, one of Lily's favorite Saturday activities and probably the one I like least. Especially at Christmas time. Especially the day after Lily announces she's falling in love.

Lily swerves into the sock department on the main floor. "Want these?" She flings a pair of glittering gold anklets in my direction. The cuffs are labeled I Love New York.

"No way!" I say.

"Let me try them," she says. Bent at the waist, she rolls pink knee socks over her own black tights.

"Lily! You'll get arrested!"

"Not me. *I* know a cop." She winks, then tosses them, inside out, onto the pile of sale stuff. Lily is drunk with love, and I just want to be alone in my room.

Ducking and darting around people and counters, we glide onto the overcrowded escalator. Squished beside her, hot as can be and unable to move my arms, I start grumbling. "Christmas shopping in this place . . . the things I do for you!"

"I have to find that battery operated makeup mirror for my mother. She *adores* presents that come in a box from Bloomingdale's," she reminds me. "And of course hand-delivered presents are best."

"Five more days and you'll be on your way to Wyoming." I sigh. "What will I do without you for two weeks?"

"Don't worry. You'll be busy enough keeping your mother away from Henry."

"Some fun," I mumble.

"Meanwhile," Lily says dreamily, "I'll be riding horses and thinking about Roger Starr." Her face is all aglow.

"Swell." I turn abruptly and head for the escalator.

On the fourth floor, Lily eases herself onto a small couch covered in gray velveteen. A lanky salesman with smooth waves of blond hair hovers nearby, watching her stroke a sample boot, red suede and very elegant.

"Size five, please." She smiles up at him.

The guy is swooning. Even as he slips on the boots, he doesn't take his eyes off her face and somehow I'm not in the mood for Lily's flirtations. Lily plays it all the way. She leans way back, swinging her leg in the air. Red suede hugs everything from toe to hip.

"What do you think?" she asks somberly.

"Not quite you," I grumble. But suddenly it all seems funny.

Sweating from his sideburns and swearing under his breath, Lily's blond spends the next five minutes prying off hip-high boots. The more flustered he gets, the harder it is not to laugh.

"Let's get out of here," I croak when Lily has finally tied her sneaker. I pull her by the arm as she blows him a Hollywood kiss. We duck behind a rack of jeans in the City Streets department and we fall in a heap on the floor, laughing.

"Donut Box is having a special," I say, after we catch our breath. "Buy six and they give you a free bag of donut holes."

"Have you forgotten? We're supposed to lay off sugar."

"If I can spend half my day shopping with you, the least you can do for me is split a bag of junk food!"

"Okay, okay."

But first she drags me through every fancy designer boutique on three. That includes the After Five Shop and the Before Five Shop, Furs By the Foot and Jeans in French. Salesladies eye us as if we're a couple of thugs on parole from the state pen. To spite them, I think, Lily spends endless time in airless changing rooms with pale curtains for doors and straight pins scattered on the floor. She models long swingy skirts and little mini ones, T-shirts that dip in the right places and silk blouses that ruffle up to her ears. And all the while, she's chattering endlessly about Roger. I sit cross-legged on the carpet, collecting pins, chewing gum, and reminding her how bored and tired I am.

Finally she is finished and we run across Third Avenue to rally on lemon-filled crullers and milk.

"My mom's going to love her new mirror," Lily bubbles on. "It's right up her alley."

"I still think you should have bought her another box of lavender stationery," I answer crankily.

Lily doesn't seem to hear me. "Roger hates donuts," she remarks, biting into her second one.

"Tsk, tsk."

"He says a single donut lays in his stomach like a lump of clay for three days!"

"What a shame." I can't help the sarcasm.

"I wish you'd quit being so unpleasant every time I mention Roger's name."

"I don't know what you're talking about."

"You're jealous, Pete. Plain jealous."

"Well let me tell *you* something," I sputter. "It would never occur to me, not in a million years, to desert my best friend just for a boy!"

"You sound like a big baby!" she shouts for all the world to hear. The waitress pouring coffee behind the counter gives us a dirty look. So does the fat lady on the other side of Lily.

"I do not!" I shout back. "Anyway, Roger Starr is in the way."

"He's not in my way. I *like* having a boyfriend. I'm not afraid of having a boyfriend. You ought to try it sometime," she adds.

My eyes are stinging and my lower lip is quivery, but I'm determined not to cry. "Boys don't interest me." I choke out the words.

Lily spins around twice. "Jon Hill interests you," she

says calmly, slapping a dollar bill on the counter. "But you're just too chicken to admit it." Then she slides off her pink leather stool and flounces out of Donut Box.

I reach for my ski jacket and punch both arms into its puffed sleeves. Outside, wet snow drops from the sky in big gray splotches. Lily and I walk on opposite sides of Fifty-ninth Street, pretending not to notice each other as we skid across town on slushy sidewalks.

Traffic, like my mood, is snarly and gridlocked. Cold beads of almost-snow make me think of the warmings up in front of Gram's marbled fireplace after sledding in Central Park . . . or running alongside my parents the time they tried to cross-country ski on The Great Lawn. Those were the days all right. The good old days.

At Madison Avenue, Lily breaks into a run. A truck grinds to a halt in the middle of the chaotic intersection, and a second later I've lost track of her. Well, fine!

At Fifth Avenue, I cross the street to warm up in the swank lobby of The Plaza Hotel. It smells of expensive perfume and mink coats. A violinist, very old and with eyes half closed, strolls by playing the drippiest love songs to tourists clinking teacups at each other.

I slump into a satiny chair. *You're jealous, Pete. Plain jealous. . . . You sound like a big baby! . . . Jon Hill interests you. . . .* The angry words spin around my head, and my stomach's in a knot, and I wish there was someone around who understood me. Up until now I thought that's what best friends were for. To understand you when no one else does. So it looks like I'm going to be in the market for a new best friend.

"I knew you'd come here." Lily struts in, shaking clumps of snow off her ski band. "Are you finished pouting?" she asks as she slips into the seat next to me.

The truth is I'm glad to see her. I guess I knew she'd walk through The Plaza, just because we always do. Best friends are like that. Pretty predictable.

All the same, I can't help blurting out, "You're a traitor, Lily!"

"Traitor?" She looks surprised.

"Yes, a traitor. Roger Starr is moving full speed ahead into your life, and I feel like I'm being dumped right out."

Lily sucks in her breath, and she puts her ice-cold hand over mine. "How many times do I have to tell you?" she asks patiently. "Boyfriends are different from girl friends, and you've got to have both."

She sounds so wise, so sure, that for a minute I almost believe her.

"Besides," she goes on as if we haven't just had the fight of our lives, "Roger says Jon says you're cute!"

I think I just quit breathing. I twist around to see if she means it. She means it all right. I can tell by the serious look on her face. *Roger says Jon says you're cute.* Funny thing is, I like the way that sounds.

No one is home when we get back to Lily's. We kick off soggy sneakers, hang our jackets on doorknobs, and head for the kitchen to make hot chocolate. A note is taped to the refrigerator.

Hi Lily.

Jake and I are at the Planetarium. Home by 4:00. I'm taking us to *Le Bœuf* tonight so don't eat too much junk food between now and then.

Love, Henry

"Dinner on the town again." Lily shrugs indifferently. "You're spoiled. Maybe he ought to take me instead. We're having Gram's stew."

Lily boils up water for our hot chocolate. "That makes two nights in a row Henry's springing for *Le Bœuf*," she says. "Of course you know he took your mom last night."

I swallow hard. "Of course," I say, wondering why in the world I believed Mom when she said she was having dinner with an old friend.

Lily carries two mugs to the table and talks quietly, almost to herself. "Henry was up before five again this morning. A fire in the fireplace. Classical music on the stereo." She circles her mug around and around, leaving a trail of wet rings. "He's so darned lovesick this time, who knows what could happen?"

"My mother's been in a great mood," I admit. "It's bad enough she's doing it, but I can't figure out why it's such a big secret. Maybe she thinks I'm too dumb to notice things like private dinner dates with my best friend's father and extra weekday jogging. . . ."

"We have to confront them, Pete."

"*We?* What about you, Lily? You're much better at figuring out grown-ups than I am."

"We have to confront them," she repeats, absently stirring her hot chocolate. "Things are getting out of hand, and we've got to stop them before it's too late."

"But how?"

"I'll think of something," she promises.

And the funny thing is, I know she will.

CHAPTER

12

"Who knows, Lily? Maybe they're just friends."

"There's no such thing as friends when it comes to grown-up people of the opposite sex."

She tosses me the rubber-tipped spatula for washing. Chocolate fudge is everywhere. On her father's COP IN THE KITCHEN apron. In the narrow space between her eyebrows. Across the length of her arm. She hands over the bowl to Jake, and he starts right in, using both sets of fingers.

"Did you get six helium balloons?" he asks. "Did you remember about purple, Lily?"

"Of course!" She checks her watch. "This is going to be the best forty-second birthday party Henry's ever had," she boasts, winking at me.

She's been planning the details, right down to the purple helium balloons, for days. For the last hour we've been putting the finishing touches on her elaborate homemade dinner. Lasagna, salad, and the chocolate cake with two layers. In fact, it's a combination birthday and farewell party. Tomorrow morning Lily and Jake are going to Wyoming for Christmas vacation.

"Will you write to Roger?" I ask.

"You bet."

"Will you write to *me?*"

"The minute I step off the plane," she promises, draping the last spinach noodle across her beautiful casserole. With the back side of a soup ladle, she spreads meat sauce on top, then sprinkles parmesan.

"This must weigh a ton!" I giggle as the two of us shove the heavy baking dish into the oven.

Lily sighs. "Too bad Roger isn't coming."

I don't say a word but thank my lucky stars Mr. Basketball has practice tonight. Frankly, I think Lily was kind of pushy to invite him. This happens to be a pretty private affair—Lily, Jake, Henry, Mom, Gram, and me.

Besides, this is a big night for another reason. Tonight Lily and I are going to watch how Henry and my mother act together. If nothing happens between them, we'll consider them innocent. But the moment they act suspicious, we're going to confront them. *We know what you two have been up to,* we will tell them in our boldest voices, *and it's got to stop! Here's a list of reasons why.*

I stare at the sheet of paper taped to the inside of one of the kitchen cabinets. The list was my idea, but it was Lily who thought up most of the eight things to put on it.

"I think I'm getting cold feet," I mumble.

"There's no time for cold feet." She closes the cabinet firmly. "Remember, *we* know what's best for Henry and your mother even if they don't."

"If you say so."

"Anyway, tonight's the easy part," she reminds me. "The hard part is Wyoming. I've *got* to make my mom see that she belongs in New York with her family. If this works, she'll have no choice but to say farewell to The Cowboy and hurry on home to us!"

"Is Mommy coming home?" Jake asks suspiciously.

"We're working on it." Lily plants a kiss on top of his head.

Lily throws a great party. In her tight black skirt slit way past her knee and the white frilled blouse with pearly buttons in back, she looks as if she just stepped out of an Italian movie magazine. Glancing down at my own faded jeans and the pink sweatshirt that used to be my mother's, I wonder why Lily can't pass on just a fraction of that chic to me.

"Delicious! Outstanding!" Mr. Rosenblume is having a wonderful time. He helps himself, and Gram, to seconds.

"Lily did everything," I brag.

"I did not!" She frowns modestly but we all know how much Lily enjoys compliments.

"I've never been very good at making parties," Mom admits. "Remember the time I tripped on Daddy's tripod, Pete, and dropped your Carvel cake all over the kitchen floor?"

"How could I forget?"

Now I'm not the sort of person who goes around looking for trouble. Everyone knows that. But something is definitely happening. It's Mr. Rosenblume and my mother and the way they keep sneaking each other these friendly little looks across the table. What a flirt Mom is.

I look at Lily. She gives me a knowing look. My palms are getting hot. *This relationship must end immediately,* I will tell them. *First of all, my mother needs to spend more time with me because I'm very nearly a teenager and . . .*

"I read about the New Year's Eve race in *The Journal* this morning," Gram is saying. "At midnight they start around the southern end of the park—four or five miles. I'll tell you one thing," she adds with authority. "That isn't the way we celebrated in my day!"

"I think it sounds neat," I say.

Lily disagrees. "New Year's ought to be a black-tie affair. Like a Fred Astaire movie."

"Why don't you and I sign up for that race, Mom? We'll have a great time," I add enthusiastically. "Just you and me."

"It does sound like fun."

"Lily and I can join you," Mr. Rosenblume suggests.

"Thanks, but no thanks." Lily's lips are pressed together. She looks at me. Probably she's thinking how nice it would be if her mother came back to the city for New Year's.

"What about me?" Jake yawns loudly. "I'm a good jogger too." He climbs onto his father's lap. Mr. Rosenblume rubs a bushy cheek against the top of his head. Jake's eyes flutter and he fights to keep them open, but in half a minute he's fast asleep.

"Looks like my team's deserting me," jokes Mr. Rosenblume. "Well, *I* will gladly run that race with you." He smiles warmly at Mom and pats her hand.

What a lot of nerve he has.

"*Farmer's Almanac* is predicting a big snowfall," Gram warns. "Do you runners run through snow?"

Lily looks down, takes three deep breaths, then nods at me. My heart is pounding. It's time. We are going to challenge them once and for all. I rub my tongue along the inside of one cheek and then the other. My palms are sweating like crazy.

She sits up tall and folds her hands on the table. She holds her head high. She begins. "Pete and I—"

"Speaking of snow," Mr. Rosenblume suddenly cuts in, clearing his throat, "I . . . we . . . wanted to mention . . ."

"Henry!" Lily says. "I was speaking . . ."

"Ellen and I are taking a ski weekend," he blurts out.

"Ski weekend?" Gram lowers her head and glares at Mom over the top of her glasses.

"Together?" I squeal, staring at Henry Rosenblume.

"We are going to Vermont." I hear Mom say those words. I hear the glimmer of an apology in her voice. Yet I haven't got the courage to look at her.

"I *suppose* there will be separate rooms." Lily's crack is mean and sharp.

"That is not your business," Mr. Rosenblume answers without moving a muscle in that cool detective face.

"You and Mrs. Jaffe are getting too close!" she yells, banging a fork on the glass table.

"That is not your business either," he yells back.

"How can you say that?" she shrieks.

"You may be a very sophisticated New York kid, Lily Rosenblume, but that doesn't give you the right to run my life!" Mr. Rosenblume is so angry his nostrils are flaring and deep lines are making creases near his eyes.

"We're a *family*," she rages on. "This is a *family* affair and what you do is *too* my business." She swallows hard, then lowers her voice to a whisper. "How can I make you understand?"

Mr. Rosenblume chews on his lower lip, staring at Lily in silence. He seems to be thinking over what she said.

"Anyway, we know what you guys have been up to," she continues, looking from Henry to Mom then back to Henry again, "and it's got to stop. Right, Pete?"

I gulp. *Ellen and I are taking a ski weekend.* I open my mouth to say something brilliant, something we've been rehearsing for days, but nothing comes out. *We are going to Vermont.* . . .

"And it's not fair." Lily looks defiantly at her father. "Because *you* belong with your wife."

Mom winces. She is very pale, and the kitchen air is heavy, like lead. Even Gram can't figure out what to say.

"Former wife." Mr. Rosenblume's voice is calm now.

"The marriage doesn't work, Lily. That part of our lives is over. It's time to go on."

But Lily is adamant. "Mom would be home in a flash, if only you needed her." Her voice cracks. "She misses us . . . so much . . ."

Suddenly I've had enough. More than enough. Pushing my chair away from the table, it falls to the floor with a crash. I don't even bother to pick it up. My only goal right now is to get out of this stifling apartment.

I take the back stairs two at a time to the ninth floor. In the delicious quiet of my room, I fall across my bed and stare at the shadowy ceiling. My heart is pounding, and my head, and I squeeze it tight, between both hands.

Later on, Mom raps on my bedroom door. Probably to tell me to quit moping. Or to tell me to quit feeling sorry for myself. Who knows, though, maybe to apologize for being such a sneak or tell me how much she needs a weekend away from it all.

"It's nice for me," she begins in her psychology voice, "to spend time with a man."

Curled on my bed, I poke a felt-tipped pen between adjacent toes.

"It's not what you think, Pete." She sits beside me.

"It's a weekend with a man!" I shout. "What should I think?"

"This does not mean for one minute that I love you less. Or your father." She says it carefully, measuring

95

each word. I bet she looked it up just now in one of those child development books. *How to Tell Your Daughter about the New Man in Your Life.*

"Then why are you sneaking around with Henry Rosenblume?" I scream. "How would Daddy feel, if he knew?"

She pulls her back up stiff and stares out the window, at the faraway lights of Fifth Avenue and the Upper East Side. Even in the darkness, I see billowy puffs of clouds rolling past. They race the wind, sailing swiftly across the city.

"He can't know, Pete," she says softly. "He's *dead.*"

Her words catch me off guard. I want to yell and punch at something. Instead I let my body collapse against hers and start to cry. She smooths my hair and rubs little circles on my back, and it feels so nice.

"How come you never told me?" I finally ask her.

"I should have. I felt so funny," she says. "I was chicken," she admits at last, handing me a tissue.

"Chicken! But you're a grown-up!"

She breaks into a tentative smile. "Anyway, I have this feeling—and I'd like to see you try to deny it—you and Lily have been snooping around like a couple of private eyes from Scotland Yard."

"You knew!" I gasp.

"Did you two think you could follow Henry and me around Central Park unnoticed?" She throws back her head and laughs. "He's a detective, Pete!"

So! They knew all along we were trailing them! I guess that's it for the Anti-Romance-Mission.

"What about those dinner dates?"

"Dinner dates," she repeats, trying to be cool.

"We're keeping track," I say smugly.

"Henry and I are good friends."

"That's not what I heard."

She frowns. "What did you hear?"

"Lily thinks maybe her father thinks he's in love again—with you, Mom." I watch for her reaction. She doesn't seem to have one. "But I keep wondering why her mother would come back to New York if Henry's in love with you."

"She isn't coming back. You heard what Henry said. The marriage doesn't work anymore."

"Are you in love with him?" I ask meekly.

"What I am," she says, sucking in her breath, "is plain happy to be defrosting after all these months. Certainly I love having Henry for a friend. Beyond that, who knows?"

"What about me?" I can't help asking. "How can you have time for a boyfriend and me too?"

Mom smiles reassuringly. "We've got to make room in our lives for new friends. But remember, Pete, nobody replaces the old ones."

Then I think about what Mr. Rosenblume said right before I left tonight. *That part of our lives is over,* he told Lily. *It's time to go on.* I guess Mom is telling me the same thing in her own way.

"So maybe you do believe in happy endings," I murmur thoughtfully. "Do you, Mom?"

She pulls me to her. "Time will tell," she answers. "Only time will tell."

CHAPTER

13

I spend my days missing Lily. I spend my nights making lists of things to tell her when she gets home from Cheyenne. So far, there are forty-seven things on my master list. I've been using Mom's old typewriter, the one she wrote the best-seller on. The forty-seventh thing on the list is a cool reminder that Lily *promised* to write the minute she stepped off the plane. So far I haven't heard a peep, even though I've written three long letters and one very short one. Eleven days and not even a postcard! Some best friend.

"It's just like old times, isn't it?" Gram says.

"Oh sure."

"Your mother and Henry aren't *eloping* this weekend." She winks pleasantly. "Just skiing."

"Very funny, Gram."

I am slouched beside her on the beige velveteen couch. Her bare feet are propped up on the coffee table in front of us, her toes freshly painted a pretty shade of red.

"Mediterranean Winter." She admires her handiwork then closes the fat issue of *Vogue*. "Go ahead, try it."

I give the bottle a good shaking. "How come you're so happy about their getaway weekend?" I demand.

"I'm just so pleased your mother is stepping out again." She wets her lips and goes on. "But I might just as well tell you, I've invited someone to dinner next Friday."

"*Someone!*" I burst out laughing. "I'd like to see the look on Mom's face when you tell her. She's going to hit the roof," I warn.

Gram pushes tiny wads of cotton between my toes as I finish painting up each one. "Your mother doesn't call me 'The Matchmaker of Park Avenue' for nothing."

"What's the poor guy's name? Prince Charming?"

"Riley. *Doctor* Riley, she says importantly. I guess I'm supposed to fall on the floor now, because he's a doctor instead of a plain regular person like Henry Rosenblume.

"Well, you better rustle up something very gourmet for The Doctor," I joke. "Maybe you can borrow the Rosenblumes' Cuisinart for the occasion!"

"I don't think Henry would care for that. I think he's the jealous type, don't you?"

On the wall across from us there's a black-and-white photo of Mom. My father took it ages ago, when they were young and graduating from college and way before I was born. Mom is typing in the picture. Her expression is sort of quiet and peaceful too. And she looks happy.

"Do you think Mom is getting happier now?"

Gram purses her lips. "You mean about Henry and the weekend? Oh yes. I'm sure she's a bit unsettled, if you know what I mean. But spending time with Henry is good for her."

"None of this would have happened, you know, if my father hadn't died."

"One of these days," she answers sternly, "you will have to stop blaming him for dying."

"I'm not too crazy about sharing my mother," I admit, "even though I like Mr. Rosenblume."

"Sharing your mother is hard work," Gram assures me as she waves the magazine like a fan across my feet. "Did the mail come yet? Any word from Lily?"

"Nope."

"Poor kid." Gram clicks her tongue. "Thinking she can go out there and patch things up . . ."

"Mom says Lily's just looking for a happy ending."

Gram nods thoughtfully. "I guess we're all doing the same thing. One way or another, just trying to carve out happy endings."

I lean over to kiss her smooth cheek. "I wish you weren't going back to Florida next week."

"I am way overdue."

"You ought to move back to New York, Gram."

"Just think what I could do for your mother's love life."

I giggle. "Eligible bachelors would be lined up in size order outside our door!"

"Okay, Pete Jaffe. You've been hanging around all weekend. It's time to get *moving!* The New Year's Eve race is creeping up on us."

"I'm not in the mood to jog. I hate doing it alone."

"It's good thinking time," she insists, giving me a friendly but not too gentle push off the couch. "Everyone needs thinking time. Even you."

So I pull on my usual layers of sweats, including long flowery underwear and the funny purple earmuffs, and head outside. As I start jogging down Central Park West, I am flooded with thoughts. Thoughts about my mother and the fact that she's coming back from Vermont this afternoon, and Lily . . . How am I supposed to know what's going on out there in the Wild West if she doesn't tell me?

All of a sudden I am bumped from behind. Bumped hard. Next thing I know, I'm sitting on cement.

"Wake up! Why don't you look where you're going?" A boy is hovering over me and he is shouting into my ear.

"Well . . . I . . ." Squinting into the late afternoon sun, I wonder for a moment if my eyes are playing tricks on me. They aren't, though. It *is* Jon Hill.

At exactly the same moment, he recognizes me too, and he quits yelling. His face burns into a nice shade of scarlet. The second cutest boy in school runs into me with his bike, and *he's* blushing like mad!

"Gosh, Pete . . . I'm sorry. . . ."

"No problem," I say in my most superior voice. "You seem to have a thing about plowing down joggers," I add. "Don't you *like* joggers?" Imagine *me* joking with a boy!

I make a move to get up, and Jon makes a move to help me. Nice! I consider suggesting an ambulance, to heighten the dramatic tension. Before I know it though, he has yanked me to my feet. It's pretty clear I am perfectly all right, all together and in one piece. Jon hands over the earmuffs that somehow wound up on his pedal. The little ring of bystanders that has gathered around us applauds, the way New Yorkers always do, then breaks up.

"So where were you going in such a hurry?" I ask, casually looking over his neat blue ski jacket with the impressive patches on the sleeve and a single bold stripe across the middle. A plaid muffler is folded twice around his neck and his jeans have just the right degree of wear. Even though I'm pretty embarrassed about the fall, I decide right then and there I like the way Jon Hill puts himself together. I like it very much.

"There's a bike shop over on West End at Seventy-second," I hear him say. "I need a new saddlebag. Want to come?"

"Why not?" I try to sound smug, like Lily. I wouldn't mind if Jon thought this sort of invitation came my way twice a day. On the other hand, as we start toward Seventy-second, I'm having a little trouble keeping my feet on the ground. Somehow I feel like flying!

On the way home, while we wait for the light at Seventieth Street, a taxi pulls up to my building. Mom steps out of the back seat.

"There's my mother! She's home!" I start to run toward her, then stop so short I nearly lose my balance. And my breath.

Henry Rosenblume steps out of the back of the cab and begins kissing her! On the lips. Right there in plain daylight. It isn't a long lingering movie kiss or anything, but there's no mistaking it's a kiss. And the worst part is Mom doesn't seem to mind a bit.

"Are you all right?" Jon wheels his bike in front of me. "You're white as a ghost."

I stand there in silence, humiliated and angry, staring at the two of them under the canopy of Number 94.

Then Jon whistles. "My parents never went around kissing in public like that!"

"My father's dead," I say slowly. "That is someone else."

He nods sympathetically. "My mom just got remarried," he confides. "She left my father when I was five." Jon has nice big blue eyes. They're friendly too, eyes that like me. I guess Lily is right again. Boys don't bite.

"You know something?" I sigh. "Grown-ups are a pain."

"I'll drink to that!" And there's something about the way he half smiles as we duck down Sixty-ninth Street. It makes me think falling in love might not be so bad after all.

"I'm training for the New Year's Eve race. I'm jogging tomorrow morning at six. Want to come?" I say it fast. Before I change my mind. Before I even think about what I'm doing.

"Six?" He laughs. "Sure. I'll meet you in your lobby." Then Jon Hill blushes. All the way up to his ears.

CHAPTER
14

Two o'clock. I am sitting on a park bench across the street from our building. For the last half hour I've been counting checker cabs. Before that I counted silver cars and before that dogs on leashes. When will Lily be here? Doesn't she know I'm bursting at the seams!

I lie back and try a dozen sit-ups with hands behind my neck and knees bent. Just as horrible as ever, but Mr. Rosenblume says they're a must for better jogging.

At last her taxi pulls up to the curb. "You're getting to be a physical fitness maniac!" Lily shouts, flying into my arms.

"You didn't even write," I scold in my friendliest tone of voice. "Forget my address or something?" I pat her short black coat. It has the nicest furry collar. Wouldn't you know, my sophisticated Lily, home from Wyoming in a new coat that makes her look eighteen. "Is that your mother's?" I ask.

Lily frowns. "I have something to tell you—"

"*I* rode a horse and also a snowplow." Jake bounces out of the taxi. "Want to see a picture of my mother, Pete?"

"She's so pretty." I admire the snapshot plastered to his sweaty hand. "Is she putting on a little weight or something?"

Mr. Rosenblume appears by the cab and then lugs two suitcases onto the sidewalk. He wraps one arm around Lily and the other around Jake. Boy, does he look happy!

Lily and I decide to stay downstairs awhile. Side by side on the bench with chipped green paint, we hook elbows and ankles. We hug and we giggle, at nothing in particular. Finally Lily turns to look me in the eye.

"I *must* talk to you. *Now.*" There's something about the way she says it that makes me think I'm in for a big surprise.

"What's wrong, Lily?"

"My mother is pregnant."

"Your mother is *pregnant*?" I shriek.

Lily nods sadly. "First she lets me know how *guilty* she feels about Jake and me. Next thing I hear, she's pregnant. I hate her guts." Lily starts to cry.

"So she isn't coming back," I murmur, hanging my arm across her shoulder.

"It hurts so much." She dips her chin into the furry collar.

"She divorced your *father*, Lily, not you." I can't believe it's me sounding so wise.

She blows her nose loudly.

"Did you tell her about my mother and Henry?" I ask, trying to change the subject.

"Not until after she told me about the baby." Lily laughs and cries into her raggedy tissue. "She said she wasn't so surprised, but *I* think she's jealous. Serves her right! By the way, Pete, she did point out that you and I could wind up sisters."

"Don't you think she's rushing things just a little bit?" I smile, though. It isn't everyday your best friend has a shot at becoming your sister.

"*I* think we'd be great sisters. We're practically that anyway, Pete. Then your mom could write a new best-seller—a hot one—about these two wonderful girls . . ."

"Jon and I saw them kissing," I interrupt.

Lily pulls in her breath. She stuffs her hands into the pockets of her new black coat. "Oh well, what's a little kiss among friends?" Her tone is flip, but I can tell she's not exactly thrilled either.

"My mother is showing healthy signs of being alive," I hear myself lecture. "It's good for her to spend time with a man—with your father."

"You sound like you almost believe what you're saying."

"I am trying to accept facts, Lily. But I don't have to like it," I add truthfully.

Lily does a double take. "Did you say you and *Jon?*" she asks, clasping both my hands in hers. *"Jon Hill?"*

I feel myself smiling from ear to ear. "You see he nearly killed me with his bike, and we got to talking and he was blushing up to his eyeballs and then he invited me to the fix-it shop to buy a saddlebag and then we passed our building just when Mom and Henry were getting back from Stowe—

"Stop!" Lily grabs both my hands. "You mean you didn't faint when he talked to you?" she teases.

"Nope."

"And you didn't duck into the nearest bathoom?"

"Nope." I click my tongue against the roof of my mouth. "I invited him to jog with me one morning."

"You *what?*" Lily's mouth drops open.

"We had a good time. We laughed a lot, Lily."

"I'm proud of you, Pete. Looks like you're going to make it after all."

The funny thing is, I think so too.

New Year's Eve. It is nearly eleven-thirty and the six of us hurry, two by two, down Central Park West. Traffic is thick, impatient, crazier than rush hour on a Friday afternoon. Faceless drivers honk angrily and giddy pedestrians dance between the cars. All around us fancy gentlemen and ladies in long mink coats and clicking high heels are dashing off to their important midnight parties.

Mom and Mr. Rosenblume are half a block ahead. They aren't holding hands, thank goodness. But they aren't walking a mile apart either. Mom's step is bouncy, and she keeps tilting her head to talk to him. Mr. Rosenblume's is a steadier, more deliberate kind of walk. He's the sort of person who knows exactly where he wants to go, figures out the most direct way to get there, and that's that. How different from my father, who walked for the fun of it, for the sheer adventure of finding a picture that needed taking!

"I can't believe I let you talk me into this," Lily complains good-naturedly.

"We wouldn't dream of leaving you behind." I wink. "Let's just call this a family affair—or something."

Behind us, Gram and Jake are swinging arms and singing Christmas tunes. It was Gram who finally convinced Mr. Rosenblume not to leave Jake behind with a sitter tonight. "New Year's in Central Park," she pleaded, "a four-year-old would remember that the rest of his life.

After the race we're all going back to our apartment. Gram has prepared nothing short of an all-out feast. Including champagne.

We go into the park at Sixty-seventh Street. The whole area is lit up like a mini–Rockefeller Center, minus the famous tree. There's an energy here, a spirit that makes me feel good all over. Vendors are everywhere. They're selling fur-lined mittens, sweet-smelling chestnuts, toasty-warm pretzels, and T-shirts labeled RUN FOR THE NEW YEAR. There's even a TV crew.

Outside Tavern On The Green, a glittery restaurant near my favorite playground, joggers are warming up. Hundreds, maybe thousands of them. Lily and I park ourselves beside a long black limousine. We begin with boring leg stretches.

"I think Jon is cute," I say.

"You've already told me that. About a hundred times!"

"Okay, okay."

"I forgot to tell you something." Lily clears her throat suspiciously.

"Well?"

"Roger and Jon are stopping by after the race. I invited them to your house," she adds sheepishly.

I stare at her in alarm. "You invited them to *my* house, Lily? What nerve! I can't believe you would—" Suddenly I stop yelling and start laughing. "I should have guessed you would pull something like this!"

"You're not mad?"

I shake my head. "Not even a little."

Just before midnight, we line up somewhere in the middle of the pack of runners. I am tingly and excited. I breathe in the icy air and let it out, gradually, in small circle-puffs, through my mouth. And way down inside my running shoes, I keep my toes wiggling. No frostbite tonight.

I nudge Lily. Mom and Henry are huddled beside each other in the front row of runners. Right now, they happen to look more like a couple of old pals than whatever else they might be. Who knows? Maybe they *are* just a couple of old pals. Probably not, though. All I know is I'm sick to death of trying to figure it out.

Anyway, Mom is a lot happier than she was a couple of months ago. Even *I* can see that. After all, my father never should have died and it's not fair. Like with Lily's parents. The fact is, they're divorced. Who says that's fair?

Suddenly Lily leans over and kisses my cheek. "Best friends?"

"Forever."

The starting horn crackles in the crisp night air.

"I've decided on my New Year's resolution," I boast as we start the course, nice and slow. "From now on I let the grown-ups in my life go about their *own* business!"

"Are you sure?" Her tone is challenging.

I pull Mom's new green ski band down around my ears and smile in the pitch-blackness.

"If you ask me," Lily says, "they could *all* stand a little help from time to time. Don't you think so, Pete?"

As we run beneath a muted street lamp, I turn to catch her grinning. Like my own Lily. My strong and wise one who understands the world so much better than I do. And I'm so glad she's home.